THE FAMOUS FIVE AND THE Z-RAYS

THE FAMOUS FIVE are Julian, Dick, George, (Georgina by rights), Anne and Timmy the dog.

A holiday in the Lake District should have meant quiet picnics, fresh air and cycling expeditions. But when a newly invented scientific device falls into the wrong hands, with possibly disastrous consequences, the Five are soon involved.

First ruthless burglars and then fanatical spies from a mysterious foreign power, determine to obtain the invention, and it is up to the Five to stop them at all costs . . .

Also available from Knight Books:

The Famous Five and the Stately Homes Gang
The Famous Five and the Mystery of the Emeralds
The Famous Five and the Missing Cheetah
The Famous Five go on Television
The Famous Five and the Golden Galleon
The Famous Five versus the Black Mask
The Famous Five in Fancy Dress
The Famous Five and the Blue Bear Mystery
The Famous Five and the Inca God
The Famous Five and the Cavalier's Treasure
The Famous Five and the Strange Legacy
The Famous Five and the Secret of the Caves
The Famous Five and the Hijackers
The Famous Five and the Strange Scientist
The Famous Five and the Knights' Treasure
The Famous Five in Deadly Danger
The Famous Five and the Pink Pearls

The Famous Five and the Z-Rays

A new adventure of the characters created by Enid Blyton, told by Claude Voilier, translated by Anthea Bell

Illustrated by Bob Harvey

KNIGHT BOOKS
Hodder and Stoughton

First published in France as Les Cinq et le Rayon Z

English language translation copyright © Hodder & Stoughton Ltd. 1987

Illustrations copyright © Hodder & Stoughton Ltd. 1987

First published in Great Britain by Knight Books 1987
Third impression 1989

British Library C.I.P.

Voilier, Claude
The Famous Five and the Z-rays: a new adventure of the characters created by Enid Blyton.
I. Title II. Harvey, Bob III. Les Cinq et le rayon Z.
English 43′.914[J] PZ7

ISBN 0-340-41709-9

The characters and situations in this book are entirely imaginary and bear no relation to any real person or actual happening.

Printed and bound in Great Britain for Hodder and Stoughton Paperbacks, a division of Hodder and Stoughton Ltd., Mill Road, Dunton Green, Sevenoaks, Kent TN13 2YA (Editorial Office: 47 Bedford Square, London WC1B 3DP) by Richard Clay Ltd, Bungay, Suffolk.

CONTENTS

Chapter One

A HOLIDAY IN THE HILLS

Anne was skipping on the garden path of Wenderby Fell Cottage. Her fair hair bounced in the breeze as she jumped up and down, swinging her rope to the rhythm of 'One, two, buckle my shoe!' She sang the words as she skipped.

Uncle Quentin had decided that as he had come to the Lake District for an important scientific conference, it would do Aunt Fanny good to have a holiday away from home in Kirrin for a change, so he had rented this pretty cottage for the Easter holidays. It was in the village of Wenderby, where the conference was being held. Of course all the children came too – George, who was really Georgina but hated her full girl's name, and her cousins Julian, Dick and Anne, who always spent the holidays with her. Last but not least, there was George's faithful dog Timmy. Timmy always went everywhere with his mistress.

They had arrived only the evening before, and as skipping was the latest craze at Anne's school, she had taken her rope out into the garden as soon as it was unpacked in the morning. 'Three, four, knock on the door!' sang Anne.

She was interrupted by footsteps running down the path towards her.

'Four, five, hurray for the Famous Five!' chanted Dick, hearing her.

'Yes, and hurray for the holidays!' said George. 'Isn't it nice to have all five of us together again!'

'Woof!' agreed Timmy.

'This looks like a fine place to spend Easter,' said Dick, looking up at the hills surrounding the cottage – or no, he remembered, he must learn to call them *fells*. Uncle Quentin had told them that hills were called fells in the Lake District, and streams were called becks. The words sounded strange at first, but the children supposed they'd soon get used to them.

'What shall we do first?' said George.

'Explore, of course!' said Julian. 'It was dark when we arrived last night, and we were tired after the long journey – but I'm feeling fine this morning!'

George looked at her cousin, the eldest of the children. He really did seem full of energy that morning. In fact they all felt the same. Perhaps it was the healthy air of the hills!

'Yes, let's start exploring *now*!' said Dick.

'Woof!' said Timmy. *He* seemed to be fizzing with energy too, in his own doggy way!

'I expect *you* want to explore Lake District rabbits and see if they're any different from Kirrin rabbits, don't you, Timmy?' said George, laughing. 'You'll be lucky if they stand still long enough for you to find out! Well, let's go and get our bicycles. It was a good idea to have them sent on ahead of us by train.'

So the Five spent the first day of their holiday exploring Wenderby village and the country round about. The village itself nestled in a valley beside the little river Wend. There were gentle hills and wooded slopes around it, where the cycling was not too steep – and beyond, the higher fells could be seen, some of them tall enough to be described as mountains.

In the evening, the children met in the bedroom which Aunt Fanny had given Julian and Dick, to talk about what they'd seen that day.

'I really like this hilly countryside!' said George. 'I'm so glad my father was asked to come to the scientific conference here!'

'George, what exactly is the conference about?' Anne asked rather timidly. 'Uncle Quentin keeps talking as if everybody knew, and I *don't*, but I didn't quite like to ask him!'

'Afraid he'd eat you up?' said George, laughing. 'His bark's worse than his bite, you know!'

Anne went red, and Julian came to his little sister's aid. 'And *you* know how stern Uncle Quentin *can* be sometimes, George! I'm sure he's lost his temper with often enough. Don't tease poor Anne! All right, Anne, I'll explain. You know that Uncle Quentin's a famous scientist, don't you? Well then, he's come here with several world-famous inventors for a conference where they'll be discussing serious scientific problems. And they chose Wenderby as the place to meet because it's so quiet and secluded here. That's better than having a conference in a busy city, where there would be reporters after them the whole time. Now do you understand?'

'Yes, thank you, Julian,' said Anne, smiling gratefully at her brother. 'And thanks to Uncle Quentin and his conference, we've got a chance to explore a part of the country where we've never been before!'

'And breathe good fresh air, and go for long bicycle rides!' said Julian. 'I expect our muscles will ache a bit at first, because the slopes are steeper than we're used to at Kirrin, but I'm sure we'll soon get used to them.'

'I'm hungry as anything after today's explorations,' said Dick. 'I wonder what Aunt Fanny's cooking for supper. I think I smell mushrooms and bacon!'

'Greedy pig!' said George. 'Don't you ever think of anything but food?'

'Of course I do, but food is very important,' Dick pointed out. 'If you're really hungry, it's hard to think of anything else!'

And the others really had to agree with him when they were sitting down to plates piled high with sausages, mushrooms, bacon and tomatoes. After supper, Uncle Quentin said he had to prepare for the conference, so he would be glad if the children would make just a little less noise than usual. In fact, they were so full of fresh air – not to mention mushrooms and bacon – that they were ready for bed quite soon, and slept soundly all night, dreaming of all the expeditions they were planning.

Next morning the weather was lovely. The sun was shining, the air was clear and the sky blue.

'Where shall we go today?' asked Dick, getting his bicycle out.

'I thought we might start along the road beside the river, going upstream, and then climb the hill up there – sorry, the fell!' said George. 'The one we passed yesterday, do you remember? The lady in the village Post Office told us it's called Sheep Fell. It didn't look as if it would be too steep for our bikes.'

'Well, if it is, we can leave them somewhere and

finish the climb on foot,' suggested Julian. 'That sounds a good idea, George. Let's be off, then.'

George's bicycle had a basket on the carrier to take Timmy when he got tired, but as he liked to stretch his legs, he started the day's expedition running along beside the children, barking happily every now and then, and looking hopefully for those interesting Lake District rabbits. What a shame that they didn't seem to want to come out and play!

The road beside the river had very little traffic on it, and it made a very pleasant bicycle ride. George and her cousins pedalled away. They were a little stiff from the cycling they had done the day before, but as Julian had predicted, that soon wore off. After a while, they turned off the road and started along another, narrower road, not much more than a path of smoothly trodden earth, which wound its way up the side of Sheep Fell. As the slope was quite gentle to start with, the children got along quite well.

The view, or rather views, since they seemed to see a new one every time they rounded a bend, were lovely. Dick was leading the way, seeing just how hard he could pedal before he began to feel tired, when something unexpected happened.

All of a sudden, Dick's bike stopped dead, as if it had come up against some obstacle in its way. Dick flew right over the handlebars, and came down with a bump on the dusty path.

Anne let out a squeal of alarm, and jumped off her own bike. George and Julian dismounted too, and ran towards Dick. Timmy had already run over to him, and was licking his face by way of showing his sympathy.

'Are you all right, Dick?' asked George.

'Did you hurt yourself?' said Anne anxiously.

Julian helped his brother to his feet. Dick struggled up, feeling himself all over in a comical way before he said, 'I think I'll survive. Oh, my poor head! I'm going to have the most enormous bump on it. Well, never mind, it could have been worse – I was lucky, really.'

'Let's go home,' said Anne, who was always rather inclined to worry. 'You've got scratches on your hands – they're bleeding a bit. We ought to wash them and put disinfectant on them.'

'Oh, don't make such a fuss, Anne!' said Dick. 'I expect there's a stream of water somewhere near, and I've got a clean hanky. That'll do the trick.'

Once she was sure her cousin hadn't really hurt himself, George was quite ready to tease him. She and Dick rather liked to make fun of each other. They both knew there was no real malice in it!

'Poor old Dick!' she said. 'I had no idea you were so clumsy – you can't even keep in your bicycle saddle any more. You're getting old, that's what it is!'

Dick was brushing himself down with the back of his hand. 'It wasn't me, it was the stupid bike,' he grumbled. 'I don't know what came over it! I was pedalling away when it just suddenly stopped. I suppose I hit a stone on the path.'

He turned his head to look at his bicycle – and the others saw a look of great surprise come over his face. Eyes wide, jaw dropping, Dick seemed staggered by what he saw.

'My *word*!' he breathed.

Julian, Dick and Anne followed the direction of his gaze, and then they too were left speechless. They had had no time to notice anything but Dick himself ever since he took his tumble, and so they hadn't yet looked at the bicycle. But now they saw what had surprised Dick so much. His bicycle was still there, in the middle of the path – but not lying on its side, as you would have expected. It was standing upright all by itself, even though it had nothing at all to lean against. It looked as if it were kept in position by some kind of magic power.

'My word!' said George, echoing her cousin.

Then she marched over to the cycle and took a good look at it, not touching it, but trying to work out how it could possibly be balancing upright like that.

'I can't see any stones at all,' she said. 'Nothing whatever for you to have hit, Dick. You seem to have bumped into – well, nothing at all!'

Dick was beginning to feel cross. He didn't like things that couldn't be explained. 'Well, it *felt* like something all right!' he said. 'I was brought up short so suddenly that I fell off the bike – and now look at it, standing there like that!'

George put out her hand and touched the handlebars. Dick's bicycle didn't fall over. It didn't even move. George gave it a gentle push. It might have been glued to the ground. She pushed again, harder, and then took hold of the handlebars and tried shaking it. For all the give in that bicycle, it might have been made of concrete!

George let go of it again. 'Well!' she said. 'Well, I never did!'

By now Dick was getting really angry, though he could hardly have said why. If he'd fallen off his bicycle, there had to be *some* reason why. And the stupid bike itself stood there as if on purpose to annoy him! He marched up to it and shook it – or tried to – with all his might. It was no use at all. There was nothing to support the bicycle, and yet it stood there balancing upright all by itself, and the children couldn't move it.

Julian went over to it in his turn, frowning. He bent down, took hold of the bicycle frame from underneath, and tried to detach it from the ground by lifting it straight up in the air. All his muscles were straining to their utmost – and still he couldn't do it. The bicycle went on standing there, upright.

'Oh, Dick!' stammered Anne, in a frightened little voice. 'Your bike is – is *paralysed*!'

In the normal way, George, Julian and Dick might have laughed at this odd remark. But 'paralysed' was just the word they would have used themselves to describe the peculiar behaviour of the bicycle. They didn't even smile.

In fact, Julian repeated what his sister had said. 'Paralysed – yes, that's exactly what it is! I can't make this out at all.'

As if he guessed there was something unusual going on, Timmy sniffed the cycle in a suspicious and interested way. The four children were baffled. They were certainly used to coming across unusual things – in fact, they were used to solving mysteries that had baffled everyone else! But a bicycle standing upright all alone, as if by magic, was more than they could begin to understand. In turn, they went on examining it and trying to shake it. All sorts of weird thoughts crossed their minds – so weird that they hardly said anything at all for fear of sounding silly! There was something here that none of them could explain. Even George, whose imagination was unusually vivid, couldn't think of any reasonable explanation to account for the paralysed bike.

Dick, who was a practical boy, suddenly said, 'You know, I think cars or at least Land Rovers come up this path. I saw tyre marks farther down. If a Land Rover comes along now it'll squash my bike flat. It's standing right in the middle of the road – and we can't move it.'

However, it was not a car or a Land Rover that suddenly came round the bend in the road – only a bicycle, ridden by a boy who looked about fifteen years old.

Seeing the group of children standing round Dick's bike, the newcomer slowed down. Once he was level with George, Julian, Dick and Anne he stopped and dismounted.

George and her cousins expected to hear him utter exclamations of amazement at the sight of the paralysed bike. However, the boy simply looked at the bike, then at the Five, and then at the bike again. Finally he reached out, tried to shake the bike, failed to move it at all, and said, without the least surprise in his voice, 'Just like mine. Well, I hope they'll believe me down in the village *now*.'

Chapter Two

THE STRANGE CASE OF THE PARALYSED BICYCLE

'*You* don't seem very surprised!' said George. 'Of course, you're quite used to seeing bicycles standing upright all by themselves, aren't you?'

The boy smiled at her. He had a frank, open face which made the Five like him at once.

'Never mind the sarcasm!' he said cheerfully.

'I'm sorry – I wasn't trying to annoy you,' she said. 'But we've been racking our brains to find some explanation for – that!'

She pointed to the bicycle.

'And you can't?' asked the boy from the village. 'Well, neither can I, but I can tell you something, though – the same kind of thing happened to me two days ago. At almost exactly this place, too.'

George, Julian, Dick and Anne all started talking at once, bombarding the newcomer with questions. He raised a hand for silence.

'Take it easy! I'll tell you all about it, but first let's get to know each other,' said the boy. 'I'm Carl Rogers – what are *you* called?'

Julian, Dick and Anne told him their names. 'And I'm George Kirrin,' said George. Seeing a glint come into Dick's eye, she decided she'd better come clean and confess to being a girl before her cousin did it for her! 'Actually, it's Georgina really, but I'd much rather you called me George – everybody does!'

'So you're a girl!' said Carl, amused. 'I might have known it!' George couldn't help laughing.

Once Timmy had been introduced they got back to the problem of the paralysed bicycle. Dick told Carl exactly what had happened to him. The big boy nodded, all the laughter gone from his face.

'Yes, almost exactly the same thing happened to me, except that I was coming down the hill and not going up. Luckily I was braking to slow myself down. All of a sudden my bike just stopped dead, like yours, and there I was, flat on the path. I was lucky not to break anything. I got up feeling furious – I was sure someone must have fixed a piece of string across the path to bring me down. I turned round – no string in sight, but there was my bicycle standing in the very middle of the path, looking for all the world as if it were laughing at me! I grabbed hold of it, I shook it – it wouldn't move an inch. And I didn't feel angry any more –

in fact, I don't mind admitting I felt pretty scared.'

Carl stopped.

'Is that all?' asked Dick. 'I mean, it looks as if you got your bike back in the end. You're riding it all right now!'

'Yes,' said Carl, 'and that's one of the oddest parts of the whole story. As I was saying, I was rooted to the spot with surprise. I didn't know what to think, or what to do. I looked all around, hoping someone would come and help me get the bicycle going again – or at least pinch me to prove that I wasn't simply dreaming.'

'And then?' asked George breathlessly.

'Well, as I was wondering what on earth to do, what do you think happened?' said Carl. 'The bike suddenly fell over sideways of its own accord. It lay there on its side with its wheels going round and round in the air. I hardly dared go near it, but everything seemed quite normal this time. I got on it again, and set off as if nothing had happened. The trouble is that when I tried telling people down in the village, they all just laughed at me and thought I was joking!'

'They won't be able to say so any more, Carl,' said Julian. 'Not when we can back up your story.'

'They'll only laugh at you too, the way they laughed at me. That's what will happen if you talk about it. I did think for a moment that if you could tell the same story, that would prove mine. But now I've had time to weigh things up, I doubt if people will believe *any* of us,' said Carl.

George was lost in thought – until she suddenly heard a loud crash.

'Look!' shouted Dick.

All of a sudden, his bicycle had fallen over. One of the wheels was still going round and round in the air. In fact, the bike looked just the way it ought to have looked at the moment of Dick's fall – twenty minutes or so before!

Anne gave a little gulp, as if she had swallowed the wrong way. Julian let out a low whistle. Dick himself stood there as if he'd been turned to stone.

Carl was looking pleased. 'I told you so!' he said. 'That's exactly what happened to *my* bicycle the other day.'

George was the first to give herself a bit of a shake and start moving again. She and Timmy went over to take a closer look at Dick's bicycle.

'I wonder if it will work the same as ever now?' she said, and took hold of the bicycle. She could pick it up quite easily, and once it was upright again it acted just like any ordinary cycle, doing whatever you wanted it to do.

'See?' said Carl, as if he were responsible for the whole peculiar incident.

But George wasn't satisfied yet.

'Well, your bike isn't paralysed any more, Dick,' she said, 'but that doesn't explain what happened.

And nobody can say it was just imagination, because we *all* saw it. Why did your bike stop so suddenly for no apparent reason? Why did it stay upright, stuck to the ground, however hard we tried to move it? And then why did it fall over of its own accord?'

'It's no use asking *me*!' said Dick.

'An absolute mystery, that's what it is,' said Carl.

'Anyone can see you don't know my cousin!' Dick told him, laughing. 'As far as George is concerned, there's no such thing as an insoluble mystery. You can bet she's already determined to solve it.'

'I imagine we're all determined to do that,' said Julian, seriously.

Carl looked from one brother to the other. 'Solve it? You must be joking,' he said.

'No, we're not,' Dick told him. 'Having adventures and solving mysteries is what we like doing best! We're not too bad at it, either,' he added, modestly.

'Carl, where exactly were you when you fell off your own bike the other day?' Julian asked the boy.

Carl pointed to a place about twenty metres down the path from where they were standing at the moment. 'There, opposite that group of trees,' he said.

'Hm. It's not very far from here,' Julian observed.

'No, it isn't.'

'Two similar incidents in the same spot can't be just chance – we'd better have a really good look round. Come on!'

And the children, with Carl's help, set off to do as Julian suggested. However, it really was a very straightforward, ordinary piece of countryside to explore. The path went up the slope of Sheep Fell in a perfectly normal way. There was a ditch beside it, and a few scrubby little bushes grew beyond the ditch on the right as you went uphill. To the left there was a drop to a ravine – not a very deep one, with brushwood growing in it. A few small trees grew here and there on the ravine side of the path.

'Hm,' said Dick, after they had looked round. 'This doesn't get us much further, does it?'

'I told you!' said Carl. 'It's an insoluble mystery.'

'*No* mystery is beyond the Five!' George assured him.

Her cousins thought that was going rather far. All the same, they weren't going to contradict her in front of a stranger. Carl said goodbye to them and cycled on downhill towards the village, and Julian, George, Dick and Anne went on uphill. But somehow they had lost interest in the expedition they'd planned – their minds were all occupied by the strange case of the paralysed bicycle!

They were quite ready to turn round and go back to Wenderby Fell Cottage for lunch – they had all agreed that it would be best to tell Uncle Quentin and Aunt Fanny about the funny thing that had happened to them that morning. Who knew – Uncle Quentin, with all his clever scientific knowledge, might be able to give them some quite simple explanation!

'We'll ask him at lunch,' said Julian. 'Uncle Quentin's usually in quite a good temper by lunch-time, always supposing no one's annoyed him in the morning, and *we* can't have annoyed him, because we've been out!'

Sure enough, Uncle Quentin seemed to be in a good mood as Aunt Fanny put lunch on the table. 'Only cold meat and salad, I'm afraid,' she said. 'I haven't had time to do any real shopping yet – but the lady in the shop down the road said she grew this lettuce in her own garden.'

It was a very good lettuce, and there was nice tender ham and cold chicken to go with it. The children weren't complaining!

As soon as Dick had taken the edge of his appetite, he broached the subject of the bicycle. 'I say, Aunt Fanny, I took a terrific tumble off my bike this morning! And then something very funny happened.'

'Oh dear, Dick – I do hope you didn't hurt

yourself!' said Aunt Fanny, rather anxiously.

'*What* very funny thing happened?' asked Uncle Quentin, helping himself to some radishes.

George took up the story of Dick's peculiar adventure, and told her father how they had met Carl from the village, who had had much the same thing happen to him a couple of days earlier.

Aunt Fanny uttered exclamations of surprise and alarm from time to time as George talked, but Uncle Quentin listened in silence, frowning slightly. He was obviously attending to every word – something you couldn't always count on with Uncle Quentin, who was rather absent-minded, but George had his whole attention at the moment. Julian, Dick and Anne waited with baited breath for him to say something, but he still kept quiet. George was too full of her story to notice anything odd in her father's behaviour.

'So then we came home!' she finished. 'What do *you* think caused it, Father? You're a scientist, so we thought you'd have some idea! Is it some kind of magnetism, do you think? Only if it was magnetism, I'd have thought it would work all the time and not just accidentally.'

George had several other ideas to suggest – all of which she could and did disprove for herself. After a while, however, she realized that she wasn't getting any reaction out of her father. 'What's the matter?' she asked rather anxiously. 'Why don't

you say something? You don't think I'm lying, do you?'

George never, never told lies, and her parents knew it. But perhaps Uncle Quentin thought she was playing a practical joke!

'Honestly, I'm telling you the exact truth!' she said earnestly.

At last Uncle Quentin opened his mouth. 'Yes, I'm sure you are,' he said. 'I'm certain it all happened exactly as you say.'

'We can all back up George's story,' Julian assured his uncle.

'Yes, we can!' said Dick and Anne.

But Uncle Quentin was still looking preoccupied – and rather worried too. He had given the children's story his full attention, and they thought his attitude was rather strange.

'Listen, all of you,' he said, sighing. 'I don't want to discuss this incident with you. In fact I'm going to ask you to promise me something – don't discuss it with *anyone*! Absolutely no one, do you understand? I want you to give me your word of honour to keep quiet about it.'

The children looked at each other in great surprise! What an extraordinary thing for Uncle Quentin to ask them. They could hardly believe it!

'Please will you give me your word of honour?' Uncle Quentin repeated. 'And please,' he added, 'don't ask me any questions. I really can't explain at the moment.'

George found her voice again. 'All right, Father. Of course we'll give you our word of honour. But why –'

'I said no questions!' Uncle Quentin told her.

'You can have *my* word of honour, Uncle Quentin,' said Anne timidly.

Dick and Julian gave him their word too, promising not to say anything about that morning's strange incident to anyone. However, Julian thought of a snag. 'What shall we do if we meet Carl again, Uncle Quentin?' he asked.

'Avoid talking about it – or even better, ask your friend Carl to promise to keep quiet too. He seems to be afraid of people laughing at him, so that should be easy enough. You said nobody in the village would believe his tale, didn't you? So much the better!'

They finished lunch in silence, all busy with their own thoughts. The children simply couldn't understand Uncle Quentin. What on earth was it all about? Why had he seemed so preoccupied? And why had he made them promise to keep quiet? It struck them that this mystery was growing bigger and stranger all the time.

Immediately after lunch, the Five went into the garden of Wenderby Fell Cottage for a council of war.

'I can't make head or tail of it,' George confessed.

'In the usual way, if we ask Father something he either loses his temper and says it's none of our business, or else he listens and gives us his advice. This time, he listened to everything we had to say, but he just wouldn't comment at all.'

'Well, there's no point in worrying any more,' said Julian sensibly. 'We've given Uncle Quentin our word not to talk about the incident of Dick's bike to anyone, so let's just forget it.'

'I think you're right, Ju,' Dick agreed. 'Let's forget about Sheep Fell and Carl and my paralysed bike, and go into the village to buy some ice cream. Nothing like a nice ice to cheer you up!' he added, laughing. 'Coming?'

So they went off to explore Wenderby village. It was quite a large village, and had several shops in it to cater for all the tourists who liked coming to the Lake District to see the beautiful scenery. You could tell which were the shops that had been part of the village for some time and which were the brand new ones catering mainly for the tourists. Some of them were probably closed all through the winter, the children decided. There was a fine church, and also a little museum of local history. The children went to look at both of them.

In fact, it was an interesting afternoon – and yet, as they went back to Wenderby Fell Cottage, the children's thoughts *would* keep straying back to their curious experiences that morning.

'Listen,' said George suddenly, putting what everyone was thinking into words. 'We can't just drop a good mystery like this! I suggest we go back to Sheep Fell tomorrow morning. I'd like to take another look at that path.'

The others agreed that there couldn't be any harm in that. They knew that as they had given Uncle Quentin their word, they really mustn't talk to outsiders about their strange experience – but that needn't stop them trying to clear up the mystery for their own satisfaction. So, next day, they retraced their steps.

'Unfortunately, Sheep Fell looked just the same as before! There was nothing they could see that looked like even the beginnings of a solution to their mystery.

'We'd better search the place again,' said Dick. 'Anyone who notices anything odd tells the others at once.'

George was walking slowly along the path, her head bent to look at the ground, when the sound of Timmy barking made her look up. Timmy was delighted! He had found a real Lake District rabbit at last – much more fun to chase than the imaginary sort. The poor rabbit was racing away as fast as it could, with Timmy after it.

'Timmy! Heel! Leave that poor rabbit alone!' shouted George.

Too late! Just then Timmy caught up with the

rabbit. Or rather, the rabbit stopped dead of its own accord, right in front of Timmy's nose.

Rather surprised by his easy victory, Timmy stopped too and sniffed the rabbit. He hadn't really meant to hurt it when he started chasing the little animal – he only wanted a game! And now, here was his quarry apparently giving in without making a good race of it. That wasn't fair! It wasn't the way rabbits usually played games with Timmy at all.

George came running up too. 'What on earth are you doing, Timmy?' she cried. 'Let the poor rabbit go!'

Timmy raised his eyes to his mistress's face. There was a very puzzled look in them.

'Timmy, old boy, whatever is it? You do look strange!' Then George bent down to look at the rabbit. 'Julian! Dick! Anne!' she called. 'Come and look at this!'

Her cousins came hurrying over. 'What is it?' they asked breathlessly.

'Look! Timmy was chasing this rabbit, and it suddenly sort of froze in front of him. It's not moving at all. Its eyes are fixed. It might be a *stuffed* rabbit – but it was running like mad a moment ago!'

'Oh, the poor thing! It's died of fright,' said Anne, tenderly. 'Timmy, how *could* you?'

She bent down, put out her hand and stroked the

rabbit. It stayed put and didn't even twitch its ears.

'Oh dear – I'm afraid it really is dead!' said Anne.

Dick bent down too and tried to pick the rabbit up, but he couldn't move it at all from where it was standing.

'My word!' he said, with a low whistle.

'It's alive all right – I can feel its heart beating. But it might as well be rooted to the ground. It's as if it had been turned to stone – paralysed. Exactly like my bicycle yesterday!'

Chapter Three

UNCLE QUENTIN EXPLAINS

'Well!' said Julian, slowly. 'What an incredible thing!'

George's eyes were sparkling with excitement.

'This is *extraordinary*!' she exclaimed. 'A bicycle yesterday – that's one thing, that was an inanimate object! But today it's a rabbit, a living creature!'

'This path's bewitched!' murmured Anne, looking timidly around her.

'Bewitched my foot!' said her sensible older brother Julian, briskly. 'All right, this is an extraordinary phenomenon, but we'll find an explanation for it sooner or later!'

George bent down to look at the rabbit too. With Timmy's interested gaze on her, she tried her hardest to pick it up. She couldn't move it so much as a hair's breadth off the ground.

Whatever the children did, the rabbit stayed

put, not moving at all, and with its eyes still fixed. It might have been made of very heavy concrete! And it stayed like that for a quarter of an hour or more. The Five didn't like to go away. They all felt as if they were waiting for something to happen, although they were not quite sure what.

'My bike finished up by un-paralysing itself yesterday,' said Dick, in an undertone.

And suddenly, so did the rabbit! The same apparently miraculous thing happened again. The rabbit's body quivered. The little creature blinked. It twitched its long ears. It let out a squeal of terror, took off as fast as it could go, and next moment it was lost from sight in the brushwood beside the path.

As for Timmy, he was so puzzled and surprised that he never thought of chasing it.

'Well, there we are again!' said Julian. 'I think this is more of a Mystery Fell than a Sheep Fell, don't you?'

'It's certainly about the oddest thing I ever came across in all my life,' agreed Dick. 'I wonder what Uncle Quentin will say when we tell him about *this*. Do you think we ought to? Will he be angry?'

Julian, as the eldest, thought the matter over and said in a firm voice, 'There's no real reason why he *should* be angry, and even if he is, yes, I think we *ought* to tell him.'

George agreed with her cousin. 'Obviously

there's more in this than meets the eye,' she said, 'and obviously my father knows more about it than he's letting on. Well, this time I think he'll have to explain! Come on, everyone, let's go home!'

George turned out to be quite right. Uncle Quentin had been spending the day at the conference, which was held in Wenderby Manor, a big country house not far from the village. When he came back that evening Julian, acting as spokesman, told him what they had seen that day.

Uncle Quentin listened to the story of the "paralysed" rabbit, and sighed.

'You've seen more than you should, children!' he told them. 'Perhaps I ought not to have brought you to Wenderby at all – I know how observant you are! Still, I wasn't to know anything like this would arise, and I hope I can rely on you. The time has come to tell you something very important, but you must remember that you've given me your word to keep quiet.'

'Of course we have, Uncle Quentin!' said Julian. 'And you know you can trust us!'

'I do, my boy, I do!' said Uncle Quentin. And then he told his story. It was a very strange story, too.

'You'll remember,' he began, 'that this conference at Wenderby is a meeting of a number of well-known inventors, who are exhibiting their latest discoveries and discussing their future uses.

One of the scientists here is called Professor Allan. You may have heard his name.'

'Oh yes,' said Julian at once. 'He was in all the papers recently, wasn't he, Uncle Quentin? Something about a remarkable scientific discovery he'd made.'

'That's right, Julian. But of course, Allan didn't say just what this discovery of his *was*. It was all expressed in rather vague terms.'

'That's natural enough,' said George. 'I suppose if you've discovered something really important you don't want to tell everyone all about it!'

'Well, children, at the first meeting of the conference yesterday, Allan told us – and by *us* I mean his colleagues, the other scientists meeting at Wenderby – just what his discovery was. He has managed to isolate a secret ray which induces paralysis and has the remarkable quality of taking effect on moving machinery as well as living creatures.'

'You mean,' breathed Anne, 'it works on bicycles *and* on little rabbits?'

Uncle Quentin smiled at Anne, who was rather a favourite of his. 'Quite right, Anne!' he said. 'Well, these rays, which Professor Allan calls Z-rays, can act selectively. I mean, in the case of a bicycle, they can stop the bicycle itself without paralysing its rider. If that happens, the rider – like Dick, yesterday – will be thrown over the handlebars. Or, they can immobilise the rider but not the bicycle. Or then again, they can immobilise both the bicycle *and* the person who is riding it.'

'Goodness!' said George, quite awestruck. 'Then this invention has a great range, hasn't it, Father?'

'Quite correct, George. It's a discovery of the utmost importance,' said Uncle Quentin. 'A living creature affected by Z-rays feels nothing while under their influence – so they can be used as an anaesthetic in hospitals, for instance, as well as for stopping criminals to escape. And there will be a great many other beneficial uses besides. You can easily imagine the military significance of the rays! The power that possesses them could immobilise the enemy's aircraft, tanks, rockets, trains, ships – even whole armies on the march!'

George frowned. Something in her father's tone of voice had caught her attention. 'Why did you say "the power that possesses them" in that funny way?' she asked. 'I mean, Professor Allan is English, isn't he? So I'd have thought his invention belonged to Britain.'

Uncle Quentin compressed his lips. 'Children,' he said, 'you've only heard the first part of my story. Now for the second – which I am afraid is rather disturbing.'

The Five pricked up their ears – including Timmy, who pricked *his* ears up quite literally.

The children could see him do it!

Uncle Quentin went on. 'When Professor Allan, who is a great friend of mine, told us about his amazing discovery, there was something else he had to tell us too. The very day before the conference opened, the small experimental transmitter he was going to use in order to demonstrate the Z-rays to us was stolen from him!'

'Ex - experimental transmitter?' asked Dick.

'Yes, the Allan Paralyser is a small metal cylinder, rather like an aerosol container. However, Professor Allan's apparatus is more complicated than an aerosol – inside, anyway. But it's quite easy to operate. The transmitter has three buttons: green, red and yellow. According to whether you press the first, the second or the third, you "paralyse" machinery – that's to say, inanimate matter – or living creatures, or both.'

'I see!' said everybody at once.

'Of course, a Paralyser for use at long range would be bigger. But Allan's small-scale model is quite adequate for demonstration purposes.'

'And it's been stolen?' asked George.

'Yes – but only the demonstration model, not the plans! That doesn't mean the disappearance of the Allan Paralyser isn't a disaster in itself. If it happened to fall into the hands of a foreign power who wanted to use it for military purposes, that foreign power's scientists would study it and might discover the secret of Professor Allan's invention. And then . . .' Uncle Quentin sighed again. However, he added, more cheerfully, 'But at least there's one thing that looks hopeful to me. Your adventures, and Carl's, seem to show that the Paralyser is *not* in the hands of any foreign power. It looks to me as if it's been stolen by some ordinary petty criminal who doesn't understand its importance.'

'What exactly makes you think that, Uncle Quentin?' asked Julian, who was very interested in the whole story.

'Well, look at it this way, my boy, your "paralysed" bicycles, and the affair of that rabbit, don't make any sense. They must be the result of clumsy use of the Paralyser by people who don't really know what it's for, and are only gradually discovering what it can do.'

George had been leaning her hot forehead against the window pane to cool it. Now she turned round. 'But why would people who didn't know anything about it steal something like that? I mean, it wouldn't look at all valuable to them, would it?'

'They could have taken it by chance, when they really meant to steal something else. You see,' Uncle Quentin explained, 'when Professor Allan arrived in Wenderby, like the rest of us, he went to stay at the Four Horseshoes Hotel, on the other side of the village. And his room was burgled! Burgled, in my opinion – and I've told you why – by local criminals, not international spies!'

George and her cousins were eager to hear all the details of the burglary. Uncle Quentin told them that as soon as Professor Allan arrived at the hotel, he decided to have a shower to refresh himself after his long journey. Before going into the bathroom, he left his briefcase, and a travelling bag containing the mini-Paralyser, side by side on his bed. He was singing at the top of his voice while he had his shower – so what with that, and the noise of the water, he wouldn't have heard any sounds in the bedroom next door. And when he came out of the bathroom again, the briefcase and the bag had both disappeared.

'Talk about absent-minded Professors!' said Dick. 'Well, careless Professors, anyway!'

'Allan didn't think there was any danger of theft, Dick,' Uncle Quentin told him. 'You see, he hadn't told anyone about the secret of his invention yet, so there was no reason for anyone to steal it. And the Paralyser itself looked very ordinary!'

Dick was busy imagining the scene. 'I suppose somebody passing by in the corridor must have heard Professor Allan singing in the shower, and opened the room door. And when he found the bedroom itself was empty, he took the briefcase off the bed, and stole the bag too, without actually knowing what it contained.'

'I'm inclined to think that's what happened too,' said Uncle Quentin. 'We can't be sure, but I believe something of the kind must account for it. In which case, the little experimental Paralyser is now in the hands of people who don't know what it really is.'

'Then it's not very serious, is it?' said Anne.

'Yes, I'm afraid it *is*, Anne,' Uncle Quentin told her. 'The thief, or thieves, are having some silly fun with that Paralyser without understanding its importance. But if they're using it like this, there's a risk that they'll attract a lot of attention and give away Professor Allan's secret.'

George jumped up from the window seat. 'So that's why you made us promise not to talk about it, Father!' she said. She began pacing up and down the room, with Timmy following her – he did look funny! 'Don't you think this scientific conference has attracted spies to Wenderby? If they discover something as odd as this is going on, they'll soon realise what's up, and then *they* will get on the track of the thief and take the Paralyser away from him. After that, they could get its contents analysed, just as you were saying, Father, and Professor Allan's invention will end up serving the purposes of some other country – maybe an enemy country! That would be terrible – somebody's got to *do* something about it!'

Uncle Quentin got up too, smiling at his impetuous daughter. 'Time for bed, children! Don't get so worked up, George. It's an alarming situation, certainly, but nothing too bad has happened yet. No news of the theft has leaked out. The local police are looking for the bag and the briefcase, and it's quite possible they'll soon track down the thief, or thieves, and Allan will have his Z-ray transmitter back.'

George and her cousins obediently went upstairs – but before going to their bedrooms, they stopped on the landing.

'I *still* think somebody besides the police ought to do something!' said George.

'Don't tell me!' said Julian, laughing at her. 'And you think that somebody ought to be us!'

'Well, *I* do – don't you, Ju?'

'I certainly think there'd be no harm in trying,' said Julian.

'Right!' said George. 'Then we go into action tomorrow!'

So next morning, the Five set out for yet another close look at the place where those extraordinary things had happened to them. They examined the path up Sheep Fell closely, hoping to find some clue, and then started exploring the shallow ravine to one side of it. This looked more hopeful. And sure enough, after they had scrambled down into the ravine, and made their way along it, they found that it opened out into a valley among the fells – and Anne was the first to notice something that seemed as if it might be interesting.

'Look!' she cried, pointing.

Dick laughed at his little sister. 'It's only a cottage, Anne!' he said. 'A ruined cottage, what's more. There can't be anyone living there, not even a burglar! When it rains the water must fall straight in.'

'It wouldn't rain much in summer, though,' said Julian thoughtfully. 'And the roof may not be quite as leaky as it seems from here.'

'Let's take a closer look,' said George.

When they came closer to the old building, they found that it stood on a small rise in the ground, set back from a minor road running through the valley. There was so much tall undergrowth and so many weeds all round the building that the children realised it could hardly be seen from the road. They had spotted it themselves only by approaching it from the other side.

'I'm not so sure it was ever meant to be a *house*,' said Julian. 'It could just have been an old barn.'

'It can't have been used for anything for donkey's years, anyway,' said Dick, disentangling a very prickly bramble from his jeans.

Timmy was already through the doorway of the little building. The children were quite close to it too, when George suddenly stopped.

'Look at that!' she said, pointing to a trail they could just make out in the grass in front of her. 'This grass has been trodden down. One or more people have been here – and more than once, I'd say.'

Dick bent down and looked at a rather muddy piece of ground. 'It was two people, I think,' he said. 'Two men, by the looks of it. I can see the remains of two men's footprints – they wore shoes of different sizes.'

'So they did!' said Anne, kneeling down beside her brother to take a look herself. 'I say! Do you think these footprints were made by the burglars?'

Chapter Four

GEORGE'S MISADVENTURE

'We can't possibly tell if the people who came here were burglars or not, just by looking at a couple of footprints!' Julian pointed out.

'We must search for some more clues,' George agreed. 'But we'd better go carefully.'

Just as the children reached the door, which was hanging half off its hinges, Timmy started barking from inside the building.

'Tim's found something!' said Dick.

Quite forgetting to "go carefully", the children hurried through the doorway.

In fact the building wasn't an old barn, but had obviously once been a farm worker's cottage of an old-fashioned kind, with one big room on the ground floor, and a loft up above. Timmy was standing in front of the fireplace in the ground floor room, barking and barking.

'Whatever is the matter, Timmy?' George asked.

'Woof! Woof!' said Timmy, wagging his tail. George went over to the fireplace and saw a little heap of cigarette ends in one corner. There were a couple of bowls and two mugs standing there too – and the mugs still held the dregs of something that looked like tea or coffee.

The children looked all round the room, but they couldn't see anything in the way of a bed. However, there was a wooden table, an old kitchen chair, and a tall wooden stool.

'It doesn't look to me as if anyone's actually living here,' said George. 'No bed – no cooking things. But obviously two people do come here from time to time. Perhaps they sit at this table, where nobody can overhear them, drinking tea and discussing their secrets. Look – there's no dust on the chair or the stool. That shows they've been used fairly recently.'

Dick went back to the doorway.

'I say!' he said. 'There's a very good view of the path up the hillside from here. Particularly the bit of the path that interests us – the place where my bicycle and that rabbit were suddenly paralysed.'

Everyone crowded to the door and looked. 'Yes,' agreed Anne. 'You can see from here without being seen.'

'In other words,' said George, 'if the two men

who seem to be using this cottage *are* the burglars who stole Professor Allan's Paralyser, they must have been using it while they were actually here!'

'Oh, my goodness!' said Anne. She sounded alarmed. 'Suppose they come back?'

'I don't think we'd better linger here too long,' Julian advised the others.

'Oh, don't be so unadventurous, Julian!' George said. 'Surely we aren't going before we've really explored this cottage? Anne, you stay on watch outside the door, and I'll go up to the loft while Julian and Dick have a good look round the ground floor room.'

Going up to the loft, however, was easier said than done. George needed a ladder to get up there – and there was no sign of a ladder anywhere.

'Bother!' she said. 'Oh, well, we'll just have to search this big room and leave it at that.'

'I don't think we're going to find anything more, you know,' Julian warned her, and he turned out to be right. The search revealed nothing. The children still had no way of knowing whether the two men who were using the old cottage were the people who had stolen the Allan Paralyser or not.

At last they set out to go back to the path on Sheep Fell, where they had left their bicycles. They saw nobody on their way. As they emerged from the ravine again, George forgot her worries for a moment and bent down to pick up a stick and throw it for Timmy.

Timmy chased after it, and brought it back in triumph. He looked so pleased with himself that George threw him another stick.

The climb up from the ravine had made the children quite hot, so Dick sat down under a tree beside the path for a rest. Anne had found an interesting caterpillar, eating a leaf on a plant in the ditch, and called Julian over to look at it and see if he knew what sort it was. But George who never stayed still if she could help it, went on playing with Timmy. He was delighted to have a good game of fetching sticks.

'Fetch, Timmy! Fetch!' George called.

'Woof!' said Timmy happily. 'Woof!'

'And here's another – fetch!'

'Woof, woof!'

Dick had closed his eyes. He was feeling a little sleepy, and heard George's voice and Timmy's barking as if they came from very far away. But then, all of a sudden, there was total silence. It was so sudden that it jerked him wide awake. He opened his eyes again and looked round.

Julian and Anne were still leaning over the ditch, studying the caterpillar. Dick looked the other way – and saw George and Timmy standing in the middle of the path. George wasn't shouting any more – and Timmy wasn't barking.

'What on earth are they doing?' Dick asked himself.

It looked like some kind of new game! George was in the position of someone running, and she had a wide smile on her face. Her hand was raised, holding a stick. But she *wasn't* running, or throwing the stick for Timmy. She just stood there perfectly still.

The puzzled dog was running round and round his little mistress, sniffing her, retreating, coming up to her and sniffing again. He looked so baffled that Dick couldn't help laughing out loud.

The noise made Timmy jump. Julian and Anne turned round to look at Dick. George still didn't move.

'What's the joke, Dick?' asked Julian.

But Dick's laughter died away. He had suddenly realised what all this meant, and a small shudder ran through him. 'Oh no!' he whispered. 'It can't be true!'

'What is it, Dick?' asked Anne, surprised.

Dick slowly raised his arm and pointed at George. 'Look at her!' he said. 'Look at George! She – *she's* paralysed too.'

Anne gave a little cry of alarm. Julian looked astonished. As for Timmy, he started barking again, and went on running round and round George, who still stood there smiling and perfectly still. Seeing that she wasn't taking any notice of him, he tried jumping up at her. Leaning both front paws on her chest, he started licking her face and whining, and then tugged at her clothes with his teeth. But both George and her clothes might have been made of stone.

Julian, Dick and Anne went over to her too. Their cousin looked as if she'd turned into a statue!

'Oh, how dreadful!' whispered Anne, with a little sob.

'It's all right, Anne, don't cry!' Julian told his sister. 'Remember what happened to that rabbit? You thought it was dead – but then it came back to life again and took off full speed ahead, none the worse for its experience!'

All the same, it was rather worrying to see George in the same state as the rabbit, and Timmy couldn't make it out at all. He kept on whining miserably as if he was sure that something terrible had happened.

Dick clenched his fists as he looked all round him, but he couldn't see anything – or anyone. 'All the same,' he muttered, 'they must be somewhere not far off, whoever they are! They're having a bit of fun by experimenting on *us*! Oh, if only Uncle Quentin was here!'

'If it really was the people who stole the transmitter who'd been using that hut, as we suspect, they must have come back there not long after we left,' Julian worked out. 'My word – we might have

run straight into them!' Seeing Dick turn his head towards the ravine, he quickly added, 'Careful, Dick! I wouldn't look that way if I were you. We don't want the thieves to guess we know where they're hiding. Remember – down there they can look up and have a perfect view of this part of the path, so we'd better be careful.'

'Yes, all right,' Dick agreed. 'But what can we do about George?'

'We can't do anything except wait,' said Julian. 'Oh, Anne, *please* don't cry! She'll soon be all right – I promise you she will!'

Anne bravely bit back her tears. She dared not look at her cousin. George's fixed eyes and the way she seemed to be running, though she wasn't moving at all, were really rather frightening.

The two boys kept watching George, but there was no change in her for what seemed like ages. 'If this goes on much longer,' said Dick, who was gradually beginning to get really worried, 'I think we'll have to go and tell Uncle Quentin and Aunt Fanny.'

'Let's wait just a few more minutes,' said Julian. 'Oh, Timmy, I do wish you'd shut up! I hate to hear you whining like that!'

Several more minutes passed by. Anne couldn't stop herself crying any longer, and burst into tears. Poor little thing, she felt miserable. Julian and Dick had stopped watching George, and kept their eyes on the ground for fear of looking towards the ruined cottage. Their enemies might still be there, watching the show and enjoying the trick they had played on the four children.

At last, the silence was suddenly broken by a furious voice.

'How dare they – how *dare* they? How dare they do a thing like that to me? They'll pay for this – they'll be very, very sorry they ever did it!'

Anne gulped. George had just "come round"!

Timmy broke into happy, excited barking. Julian and Dick felt enormously relieved. They clapped George on the back!

'George, thank goodness! You're back with us again!' said Julian.

'And perfectly all right, too,' said Dick happily.

'Is *that* all you can find to say?' George exploded. She was still in a furious temper. 'I suppose you thought I looked very funny, rooted to the spot like that just when I was running with a stick to throw for Timmy! But I was conscious all the time, you know! I could hear everything you were saying, and I could see you when you walked in front of me. On the other hand, when Timmy licked me I couldn't feel anything at all. It really was like being turned into a stone statue.'

Anne hugged George. 'Oh, I was so scared!' she said. She still felt very upset.

'I wasn't exactly enjoying myself,' said George.

'Those dreadful men! Fancy choosing you to try out the Z-rays!' Anne went on.

'I promise you they'll be sorry!' said George, grimly.

Dick couldn't help laughing at her fierce tone of voice. 'I wouldn't want to be in *their* shoes if you manage to track them down.'

'You certainly wouldn't! I shan't forget I've got a score to settle!' George assured him.

Julian was nodding thoughtfully. 'I wonder what Uncle Quentin will say about *this*?' he remarked. 'I think we'd better get home as fast as we can and tell him.'

The children mounted their bicycles, and set off back to Wenderby Fell Cottage. Timmy ran ahead of them all – he was both delighted to have his mistress back to normal, and anxious to get away from the place where they had had such a nasty experience.

Now that they were feeling better about it, Julian, Dick and Anne were full of questions they wanted to ask George. But George herself hadn't got over her misadventure well enough to think of anything but the revenge she hoped to have on the people who had reduced her to such a state of helplessness. It was rather humiliating, too, to have been used as a subject for one of their experiments.

Aunt Fanny and Uncle Quentin reacted in different ways when they had been told the story.

Poor Aunt Fanny was horrified to think of such a thing happening to George, while Uncle Quentin was particularly interested to discover that George had been fully conscious all the time she was "paralysed".

'That's a most valuable piece of evidence to add to what we already know of the effects of the Allan Paralyser!' he told the children, sounding quite excited. 'You see, the Z-rays have never been tried out on a human being before.'

'I'd just as soon they hadn't been tried out on our daughter!' remarked Aunt Fanny, but Uncle Quentin took no notice of her.

'Thanks to you, George, science has taken a great step forward!' he said.

George herself was not too keen on helping science take great steps forward either. What she wanted was revenge! However, the children decided it would be too risky to go back to the tumbledown cottage that day.

'If the thieves are still there, and they see us coming back, they'll make off – and what's more, they'll realise we're on their trail,' Julian pointed out. 'However, I think we could go back tomorrow. What we'd better do is take turns keeping watch on the place. If there's one of us hiding nearby all the time, it'll be very bad luck if we don't manage to find out more about them.'

George was not at all happy about the idea of

postponing action, even for half a day – she was someone who liked to tackle a job directly. But she saw the sense in what Julian said, and waited as patiently as she could until next day.

And next morning, it turned out that there had been an interesting new development overnight.

Chapter Five

THE MASKED MEN

'The milk's rather late this morning,' said Aunt Fanny, pouring what was left into a jug. Just at that moment, however, the milk float came down the road and drew up outside Wenderby Fell Cottage. 'Oh, children, would one of you just pop out and ask the milk lady for an extra pint today? We seem to be drinking more milk than usual up here in the healthy Lake District air!'

George, Julian, Dick and Anne were very ready to help Aunt Fanny, so they *all* ran out to ask for the extra pint – and they were pleased they had done too, because the milk lady had a very interesting story to tell.

'Sorry, I'm late,' she said cheerfully, 'but everyone wants to stop and talk about the news today!'

'What news?' asked Julian.

'Why, didn't you hear? There's been a break-in,

up at Blackmore's Farm.'

'A break-in?' said the children, all together.

'Oh, please, tell us about it!' said George.

The milk lady smiled at her eager voice. 'Well, it was two men who broke into the farmhouse. When everyone had gone to bed, they forced the door and broke in. Mr and Mrs Blackmore, the farmer and his wife, were already asleep. They were woken up all of a sudden when the lights came on.'

'The *lights*?' said Dick, surprised.

'That's right – the burglars just switched the lights on, bold as you please, and there they were in the bedroom doorway!'

'They can't have cared if they were recognised, then,' said Julian. 'So I suppose they weren't local people?'

'Well, as to that, nobody knows,' said the milk lady. 'The fact is, the Blackmores couldn't identify them even if they saw them again, because they were wearing stocking masks. You can't make a man's face out through one of them.'

'So obviously they didn't mind if they were seen or not,' said Anne, nodding.

Dick was anxious to hear the rest of the story. 'Go on!' he said. 'What happened next?'

'These two men said they wanted all the money and valuables in the house – but Mr Blackmore's no coward, not he, and he wasn't letting them get away with that! He jumped out of bed and picked up the shotgun he always keeps by his bed at night, right to hand – the farm's a good way from the village, you see, and Blackmore's a sensible, careful man.'

'Then what?' asked George.

'That's where the story becomes very strange,' said the milk lady, who obviously enjoyed a good gossip. No wonder she had been late delivering the milk that morning! 'If it wasn't the Blackmores, I'd hardly believe it, but they've got their heads screwed on all right, they have, and wouldn't go making such a tale up. It seems that just as Mr Blackmore was raising his gun, one of the burglars pointed something at him – looked as if it might have been an aerosol can, or a small fire extinguisher, or the like, from what the Blackmores say. Well, the burglar pressed a button, and all of a sudden Mr Blackmore couldn't move. It was as if he'd been turned to stone! And that's not all. Poor Mrs Blackmore, terrified out of her wits, started screaming. And then there *she* was too, unable to move, stuck with her mouth wide open and one leg half out of bed. The farmer and his wife both stayed there like that for almost half an hour!'

The children exchanged meaningful glances. What the milk lady and the other villagers must be thinking of as a strange, uncanny story, was only too obviously another example of the effects of the Allan Paralyser! The two men who had stolen the transmitter must have found out exactly what it could do – and now they were using it for their own dishonest purposes. Very likely the papers would soon be full of their crimes!

Unaware of the thoughts going through her hearers' heads, the milk lady went on with her story.

'So the two burglars calmly ransacked the house and set off again, cool as you please! Ten minutes later the Blackmores found they could move again. Dear me – I mustn't stand here talking, though! There's a lot of people still waiting for their milk. That's the news this morning, my dears – nobody knows *what* to make of it! Goodbye!'

And the milk lady got into her float and went off down the road again.

'*We* know what to make of it!' said George.

'Yes. This could be only the first in a whole series of burglaries,' said Julian, frowning. 'I'll just take the milk in to Aunt Fanny, and then let's go into the garden and discuss the situation.'

A few minutes later, the children were sitting on the grass at the end of the cottage garden, basking in the spring sunlight as they talked.

'Things are getting rather serious, aren't they?' said George, thoughtfully chewing a blade of grass. 'Not only have the men who stole Professor Allan's transmitter discovered exactly how to use it, so they can go about committing crimes and get away scot-free, but the transmitter itself has been seen and its appearance described. It'll get into the papers, and soon everyone will know the secret!'

'What can we do, though?' asked Anne, rather alarmed by the speed with which things had started to happen.

'We'll keep watch on that ruined cottage, for a start,' said George. 'Taking turns, just as we'd planned. In fact, I think we ought to have someone on duty there day *and* night.'

'Night?' said Julian, frowning. 'I'm not so sure about that, George. Aunt Fanny and Uncle Quentin wouldn't like the idea.'

'We don't have to tell them, do we?' said George rather impatiently.

Julian still wasn't happy. 'I don't like being deceitful,' he said.

'It's not being deceitful just to say nothing,' George protested. 'Anyway, the end justifies the means!'

It took her a little more persuasion to bring Julian round to her way of thinking – but she had Dick on her side too, and in the end Julian agreed, though rather reluctantly. He insisted, though, that they must at least keep watch in pairs at night. He wasn't going to have the younger children out there in the dark all on their own.

It proved impossible to carry out the plan of keeping watch on the old cottage at *all* times of the day and night! The children took turns, and while it wasn't difficult to be away from Wenderby Fell Cottage at lunchtime if they said they were going for a picnic, they all had to put in an appearance at supper, or Aunt Fanny and Uncle Quentin would certainly have wondered why someone was missing. So, although whichever couple of children was next on duty could slip out of the house after supper, there was a gap of about two hours during which no one was on watch. And of course, the four cousins kept wondering if it wasn't at exactly that time of day the two burglars visited their hide-out.

They began to suspect this more and more strongly as two nights and three days went by, and still they had seen no one visit the ruin. Meanwhile, just as they had expected, more and more burglaries were being committed locally. The "masked men", as the newspapers called them, were on a positive burglary spree! They always worked in the same way – disguised by their stocking masks, they broke into farmhouses without even bothering to keep quiet about it. If they disturbed anyone, they simply turned that mysterious cylindrical object on them, and they would be immobilised at once, unable to move for twenty minutes or more. Once these unfortunate folk *could* move again, it was too late to run after the burglars. The thieves' strange weapon had struck terror into the whole countryside round about –

and how could they ever be identified, when no one had seen their faces?

George was getting angrier and angrier. On the third evening, she told the others, 'We can't go on like this! If nothing happens tonight – well, I'm jolly well going to keep watch from seven to nine tomorrow evening! I'm sure that must be when they come to their hide-out.'

'But how will we explain it to Aunt Fanny and Uncle Quentin if you aren't in for supper?' asked Dick.

'I don't know and I don't care!' said George. 'I just want to catch those thieves at it – all by myself if I must, and I don't mind if it *is* dangerous!'

Her cousins knew it was no good arguing with George when she was in that sort of mood. Julian just hoped something *would* happen tonight, before she could put her rash plan into action.

He and Anne were on duty in the ravine from nine till eleven that evening. George, Dick and Timmy were coming to take over from them then. They made their way quietly out of Wenderby Fell Cottage, and as they cycled off towards Sheep Fell to start their watch, they passed a farm which was set some way back from the road.

George and Dick might not even have noticed it, if its darkened windows hadn't suddenly lit up just as they were bicycling by. And then someone started shouting – and stopped again almost at once. There was silence again.

The two cousins had both stopped to listen.

'Let's leave our cycles here and go and take a look!' said George. 'That sounded very suspicious to me.'

'Another farm being attacked by the masked men, do you think?' asked Dick in a low voice.

George nodded. The same thing had occurred to them both. They made their way quietly up to the farmhouse, followed by Timmy. It was a dark night, so they could get into the farmyard without meeting anyone. Quietly and cautiously, they went over to a tractor standing near the back door of the house and flattened themselves against it. Then they listened. An unexpected sound reached their ears. It came from one of the lighted upstairs windows – the sound of laughter!

A moment later, the children heard heavy footsteps coming down the farmhouse stairs. Two men came out of the house, chuckling to themselves. George and Dick saw them pull off the masks they wore, but unfortunately it was too dark for the children to be able to see their faces. They were carrying a large bag, which looked heavy, and they were still laughing.

'We made a pretty good haul tonight!' said one of them. 'To see those poor fools, standing there like statues! Ha! Did you see their faces?'

'Side-splitting, it was!' his companion agreed.

'Very useful, that little device, in a job like ours.'

So George and Dick had guessed right! They had witnessed one of the raids carried out by the men who were terrorising the countryside. It was rather frightening to be so close! Here were the Five, looking for the people who had stolen the transmitter, and now not only the men themselves but the Allan Paralyser too must be right under their noses. However, what could they actually *do* about it? Of course, George thought, she could order Timmy to attack one of the men while she and Dick went for the other one. But the odds would be against the two children, for these were big, heavy men, and there was no way of telling which one carried the Paralyser. He might get it out and use it before they could even reach him.

Dick too realised there was not much they could do. Really, it was infuriating! Timmy's hair was bristling – he was only waiting for George to give the word, and he would have gone into the attack. But to the dog's great surprise, George let the thieves get a good start.

'Now let's follow them!' she whispered to Dick. 'And mind you keep quiet, Timmy!'

There really wasn't anything else to do – Dick quite saw that. He set off after his cousin and Timmy down the long path from the farmhouse to the road.

Once the two burglars reached the road, they

went to two motorbikes which were leaning against a tree.

'Oh no!' Dick groaned quietly. 'They've got motor transport!'

George was more optimistic. 'They haven't noticed our bikes, though – that's lucky. Come on, Dick! They're making for Sheep Fell. I bet they're on their way to the ruined cottage.'

She, Timmy and Dick set off as fast as they could go. They had the noise of the motorbike engines to guide them, though it was fading as the two men got further away. But it was enough to lead them, just as George had guessed, to the ravine.

As soon as they arrived, George and Dick almost bumped into Julian and Anne, who were breathless with excitement.

'We've done it!' said Julian triumphantly. 'The thieves are here at last – inside the ruin!'

'We know,' gasped Dick, out of breath. 'We've just seen them burgle a farmhouse – we followed them here.'

'You *saw* them at work?' said Julian. 'Then we'd better go straight to the village and tell the police!'

'Wait a minute,' said George. 'We ought to think this out first. Our birds could have flown by the time the police get here. And another thing – it strikes me the priority is to try to get the Allan Paralyser back.'

'Don't be silly, George,' said Julian. 'That could

be dangerous.'

'Nothing venture, nothing win!' said George. 'And remember what an important discovery that transmitter is.'

'Yes, I know, but –'

'Oh, *Ju*, must you be so down-to-earth all the time?' cried George impatiently. 'But this is no time for arguing! Look – why don't we split up? Julian's very fast on a bike, so he could ride off to the police station and come back with reinforcements. And Anne, you go back to Wenderby Fell Cottage and tell my father. Dick and Timmy and I will stay here. Go on, you two – hurry!'

It was true that there was no time to be lost, as even Julian realised. In this serious situation, he took a quick decision, and said he would fall in with George's plan. So he and Anne set off, riding their bicycles back to the village.

As soon as they had left, George and Dick crept closer to the ruined cottage, with Timmy on their heels. They saw a faint light inside.

'Careful!' whispered Dick. 'There's one of the men coming out!'

They watched a shadowy figure making for a small tumbledown shed beside the old cottage. It was surrounded by such tall weeds that the children had hardly noticed it before. The shadowy figure went in, and came out again carrying something which showed up clearly in the moonlight as the moon came out from behind a cloud.

'It's a small, folding metal ladder!' George exclaimed in an undertone. 'What an idiot I am! I never thought of looking for a ladder in that old shed the other day!'

The man went back into the ruined cottage, but very soon came out again, followed by his accomplice. They put the folding ladder back in the shed, and then went off, away from the ravine.

'The police aren't going to get here in time!' breathed Dick. 'Julian can't even have reached the village yet.'

'Ssh!' whispered George. 'Better wait a moment longer.'

When the sound of the motorbikes had died away, she came out of hiding, and made for the cottage. 'Come on, Dick!' she exclaimed. 'They didn't have that bag with them when they left! I'm sure it contains tonight's haul – and maybe the Allan Paralyser too. It must be in the loft. Come and help me with the ladder!'

Dick shook his head rather doubtfully. 'I'm not so sure,' he said. 'Don't forget, these men have burgled several farmhouses over the last three days, and we haven't found them here ever before!'

'Well, I suppose they have several other hide-outs as well as this old cottage. They're clever. They don't want to risk being seen too often in the same part of the countryside.'

Dick wasn't really convinced by his cousin's argument, but he knew George sometimes had brainwaves! She *could* be right. Anyway, he helped her with the little, lightweight aluminium ladder, and the two cousins went into the cottage.

Once they were inside, they had to switch on the torches they had with them so they could see. The place looked just as it had before. There was no sign of the bag and its contents in the ground floor room. George put the ladder up to the opening of the loft, and nimbly climbed it.

Almost at once, she cried, 'I was right, Dick! The bag's here, half hidden under some straw!'

Dick hurried up the ladder after his cousin, and helped her down with the big, heavy bag. George emptied its contents on the table. The first thing she saw was a small grey cylindrical object with three buttons on it – one green, one red and one yellow!

'The Allan Paralyser!' breathed Dick, awe-struck.

'I told you so!' said George triumphantly.

This was the find they'd really hoped for – however, they didn't forget to look at the rest of the contents of the bag as well. There was a good deal of money, some jewellery which didn't look particularly valuable, a radio and a rather nice camera.

Then, all of a sudden, Timmy began growling. George looked up, trying to see into the darkness beyond the broken window panes.

'It must be the police!' said Dick. 'That was quick!'

But now Timmy started growling. Almost at once, two figures appeared in the doorway – and they were not policemen. The two men stood there scowling at the children.

'You see?' one of them told his companion. 'I *said* there was someone spying on us out there. I thought I heard something moving when I went to get the ladder, and I was right!'

'It's only a couple of kids,' said the other man.

'Only a couple of kids who happen to have found our hiding place! They'll be sorry about that. A lucky thing we were on our guard!' And the man who had been speaking brought a knife out. 'I'll start on the dog, and then we'll decide what to do with this precious pair!'

However, Timmy had no intention of letting anyone "start on" him. He was gathering himself to leap for the man's throat when George quickly ordered, 'Sit, Timmy! Don't move. Sit!'

Dick was baffled. He had been taken by surprise when the man came back, and couldn't think what to do next. But to his amazement, he saw that his cousin was actually smiling.

'Trying to threaten us, are you?' she asked the

man in friendly tones. 'You know, I don't think that's very nice of you! Didn't they teach you any manners when you were at school?'

The two men stared at her, open-mouthed.

'Now, perhaps you'll be kind enough to drop that knife,' George went on. 'Because if you don't, something very, very nasty will happen to you.'

The man who was threatening Timmy seemed to recover from his surprise. He took a step forward, still holding his knife. George laughed, snatched up the grey cylinder – and pressed the red button.

Caught straight in the path of the Z-rays it emitted, the two thieves were rooted to the ground at once – much to Dick's relief.

'I say, that was quick thinking!' he said. 'Well done, George. Quick work, too! Congratulations on your reflexes!'

George was beaming happily. At last she had had her revenge! And what a revenge, too! Under the very noses of the furious but helpless thieves, the two cousins put the stolen items back in the bag, while Timmy ran round and round the two motionless men. He really looked as if he was making fun of them! You could have said he was sharing in his mistress's moment of triumph.

Suddenly the two children heard the sound of car engines out in the road. Car doors slammed. And a few moments later, the police and Uncle

Quentin arrived. Julian and Anne had guided them to the spot.

It was a great moment. As soon as the thieves came out of their "paralysed" state, the police put them in handcuffs. The men were so demoralised that they confessed to having several hiding places in different parts of the local countryside, just as George had guessed. The things they had stolen were hidden there, and could easily be recovered.

The police sergeant in charge of the operation congratulated the children warmly.

'I'll just drop in at the farm these two villains burgled this evening, to tell the people there that all's well,' he said. 'After that I'll see this precious pair safely locked up in the cells.' Then he turned to Uncle Quentin. 'Now, sir, I understand you don't want any publicity about this – er – extraordinary device! A Z-ray transmitter, you said? Never heard of it! Well, this isn't exactly within police regulations, but all the same I think I'll leave it to you to hand it back to its rightful owner.'

'I'll do just that, without a moment's delay!' Uncle Quentin assured the sergeant. 'Although I'm afraid there have been so many leaks of information already, it's not much use trying to keep the thing secret any longer. Every country in the world must know about Professor Allan's invention by now. I'll be anxious to have it out of my hands as soon as possible, Sergeant. And once

Allan has it back, he'll have to be extremely careful if he wants to keep it in his possession. The fact is, my distinguished colleague is a leading light in his scientific field. But like so many brilliant scientists, he can be shockingly careless at times.' The children couldn't help grinning secretly at this – they knew how forgetful and absent-minded Uncle Quentin himself could be! 'I shall have to persuade him to exercise the utmost caution,' he finished.

While the police took the two men they had arrested off to the cells, Uncle Quentin drove the children back to the village in his car. The police had taken George's and Dick's bicycles in their own van, saying they would drop them off on the way to the police station. George had to listen to a lecture from her father as they drove home.

'Sometimes I really don't know what comes over you, George. How could you go dragging your cousins into something of that sort, which meant all of you running such risks?'

It was as much as gentle little Anne could do to make peace between them!

Professor Allan, as the children knew, was staying at the Four Horseshoes Hotel, a very comfortable place on the far side of Wenderby village. Uncle Quentin planned to go in and knock quietly at his fellow scientist's door, hand him back the Paralyser, and be off again with the children. He didn't want any more fuss or publicity about the precious transmitter.

But much to his surprise and annoyance, when he drew up outside the Four Horseshoes, instead of finding the hotel in near darkness, with its guests either already asleep or on their way to bed, all its lights were blazing, and it was obvious that the place was in a state of great excitement.

'Goodness – look at that!' exclaimed Julian. 'What on earth is going on?'

Chapter Six

PROFESSOR ALLAN IS MISSING

Uncle Quentin and the Five jumped out of the car and went into the hotel. They found the manager in the lobby. He looked very pale and upset, and he was practically wringing his hands. Several of the other scientists who were staying there, like Professor Allan, were crowding around him. Some of them were still in their daytime clothes, but others were wearing dressing gowns, and they all seemed to be in a state of great excitement. The night porter, who was very upset himself, kept talking to the people who were bombarding him with questions. 'Like I said – these two gentlemen came to see the Professor! Very distinguished sort of gentlemen they seemed. I saw them come downstairs with the Professor – poor man, he didn't look at all well!'

Uncle Quentin interrupted the porter. 'What

Professor?' he asked.

The man turned to look at him. 'Why, Professor Allan, sir!'

'Oh, there you are, Kirrin!' said one of the scientists, coming over to Uncle Quentin. 'What a shocking thing this is! Professor Allan's disappeared – I wanted to consult him on a point for tomorrow's session, so knowing he goes to bed late I went to knock on his door. I found it open, and there was no one inside. In fact, Allan wasn't anywhere around. I waited there for a few moments, and then I began to feel worried. So in the end, realising he wasn't coming back, I roused the manager here. I'm very much afraid Allan's been kidnapped.'

Uncle Quentin and the children tried to find out more details, and the night porter gave them the story. Two very polite and very well dressed men had come to the reception desk. They said they had an appointment to see Professor Allan. So the night porter, whose name was Fredericks, had told them his room number. Not long afterwards they came downstairs again, supporting Professor Allan between them. He seemed to be rather dazed, and was having trouble walking.

'I'm afraid our friend here has been taken ill,' one of the visitors explained. 'We're taking him to hospital. Don't worry – we'll let you know how he's doing tomorrow.'

The night porter had let them go off with the Professor. 'But I didn't quite like it,' he explained. 'I told myself they could just as well have called a doctor to come here and see him. There was something funny about it, taking the poor Professor off like that. After a while, I thought I'd just set my own mind at rest, so I rang the hospital, and Professor Allan wasn't there. They knew nothing about it at the hospital at all! I'd just hung up when this gentleman here came to ask me if I knew where his friend the Professor might be. So then I roused the manager.'

'I didn't like the sound of it either,' said the manager. 'And now I'm sure there's been a kidnapping. A kidnapping here, in this hotel! Oh dear – my professional reputation will be ruined!'

'Never mind your professional reputation for the moment,' said Uncle Quentin rather testily. 'Tell us what you've done by way of finding our colleague!'

'Naturally I have called the police, sir!' said the manager, stiffly.

'The police?' asked Dick.

'Yes, young man, the police, to be sure! I made a telephone call to town, and two police detectives will be here any minute. Meanwhile, they assured me, every precaution would be taken. There are roadblocks being set up, and the police are watching all the sea and airports.'

It was only obvious that foreign spies had read the newspaper stories about the theft of Professor Allan's briefcase and bag, heard reports of the local burglaries, and putting two and two together, they had realised there was a secret invention involved. So two emissaries of a foreign power must have come to kidnap the scientist, in order to get hold of his secret!

'The nearest international airport is only thirty miles away,' said the hotel manager. 'Your friend was kidnapped scarcely half an hour ago. But driving fast, the kidnappers could have reached the airport within that half an hour.'

'You're right,' agreed one of the scientists. 'They may have got him on board a plane before the police alert could go out.'

'It all depends just where they were going,' said someone else.

George turned to the night porter. 'Were they in a car?' she asked.

'Oh, yes,' the man told her. 'I went as far as the door with them. They had a big black car parked just outside – looked like a foreign one to me.'

'Mm – that's not much of a description to go on,' said George, almost to herself. 'And you say the Professor looked ill?' she asked the porter.

'Oh yes, miss, he did. His head was lolling about, and the other two men practically had to carry him. All three of them got into the car, and it set off at once.'

'Did you see which way it was going?' asked Julian.

'They went off westward – that's the road that would have taken them to the airport, if they were bound for it,' said the night porter. 'They certainly started off that way. I saw that all right.'

Julian had almost forgotten there were any grown-ups present, he was getting so interested in the mystery of Professor Allan's disappearance. He turned to discuss it with the other children. 'It looks very much as if the Professor was drugged by his kidnappers,' he said in an undertone.

'This is terrible!' whispered Anne. 'Oh, poor Professor Allan! What will they do to him?'

'They'll try to make him tell the formula for his Paralyser, of course,' Dick told his sister.

George had been thinking things out. 'Once they got to know about the Paralyser, they didn't even bother to look for the thieves who had stolen it so as to get their own hands on it,' she said. 'They kidnapped the inventor himself rather than trying to get hold of his invention.'

'We can only hope the police, or the Secret Service, or whoever deals with this sort of thing, will find the Professor soon,' said Julian.

George said no more. *She* was wondering whether the spies and Professor Allan had reached the airport before the alarm was raised or not.

She was still wondering when she woke up next morning. The children listened to the radio news while they had their breakfast. Of course, the main news item today was the kidnapping of Professor Allan. Unfortunately nothing more was known of the whereabouts of the Professor and his kidnappers. A big police search had been mounted, but no trace of the three men had yet been found. Interpol had been called in, and sea and airports outside the country as well as in the British Isles were on the alert, but there were no reports of any suspect travellers. The inventor of the Allan Paralyser might have vanished into thin air.

As the children sat in a sunny hillside meadow that morning, they looked at the problem from every angle they could think of. Munching a blade of grass, her arm round Timmy's neck, George summed up the situation as she saw it.

'If we're to believe what the newspapers and the radio say,' she said, 'Professor Allan can't have left the country. *I* don't think he's been taken abroad yet, either. In fact I think he's very probably still in the Lake District.'

'What makes you think that, George?' asked Dick, puzzled.

George threw her blade of grass away and explained. Her eyes were shining with enthusiasm as she told the others her theory. 'Well, it's like this. The men who kidnapped the Professor would have wanted to cover up their tracks very fast. I know there's an airport only thirty miles away, but supposing the Professor's disappearance had been reported to the police early enough, they risked arrest as soon as they got there. And it's quite likely there was more than *one* set of foreign Secret Service people after Professor Allan. So the ones who actually got him may well have worked it out that if their rivals, the other Secret Service men, thought they'd whisked him straight out of the country, they'd be safer lying low in England for the time being.'

'You may have a point there, George,' said Julian. 'But it doesn't get us much further, does it?'

'Well, of course I'm not *sure* that I'm right, and that the men are still around these parts,' George admitted. 'If they did get out of the country fast enough to escape the police hunt for them, then there's no hope that we can do anything. But if there's any chance at all that they may be lying low in the Lake District – and I've said why I think there *is* at least a chance of that – why don't we try looking for them?'

'There certainly wouldn't be any harm in that,' agreed Julian. 'But don't forget, the police are looking for them already!'

'That doesn't mean we can't mount a search of our own!'

'But where would we search?' asked Anne.

'You remember that Fredericks, the night porter, said he saw the black car set off westwards, along the road that would eventually have led to the airport? Well, that's the direction we ought to concentrate on. And for a start, we could try to reconstruct the black car's journey. Somebody may have seen it driving by.'

'The police will have asked that sort of question already,' Julian reminded her. 'And obviously they drew a blank, since the radio news said nothing about it.'

George waved her cousin's objections away.

'Yes, I know, Ju, but we just *might* come across some detail that's escaped the notice of the police. And they don't always tell everything on the radio, you know! Anyway, it's worth trying.'

After discussing George's idea for a little longer, the children all agreed it was possible the kidnappers *had* gone to ground in the Lake District, as much with the idea of pulling the wool over the eyes of anyone else interested in the Professor as of evading the police.

'If Professor Allan really is being kept somewhere near here,' said Julian, rising to his feet to go and pick up his bicycle, 'it must be in a house somewhere. Either a house belonging to local people, or one that's been rented recently by strangers to the area.'

'We can rule out local people,' George said, as

she too got to her feet. 'They'd have to be accomplices of the kidnappers, which isn't at all likely. Remember, it's the newspaper stories about the mysterious events here that will have attracted the spies to Wenderby in the first place. This must be the first time they've actually been here – they wouldn't *know* any local people.'

'Then we ought to find out about properties hired out to visitors over the last few days,' said Dick. 'Preferably houses in some remote place –

Dick was interrupted by an exclamation from Julian. 'Oh no! I've got a puncture!' He took a good look at his front wheel. 'The inner tube of that tyre's been patched up so much, I think I'll really have to buy a new one. It's a good thing the garage isn't far off.'

As there was no cycle shop in Wenderby, the garage on the corner sold spare parts for bicycles. The Five set off, all the others wheeling their bikes to keep Julian company.

When they reached the garage, the petrol pump attendant was busy filling up a customer's car. He knew the children by sight, and gave them a cheery wave. 'Hallo there – what can I do for you?' he asked.

'I need a new inner tube,' Julian explained.

'I'll be with you in a minute. Just let me give my customer his change, and I'll find your tube for you.'

He was as good as his word, and was soon taking the flat tyre off the bicycle wheel, talking to the children as he did so.

'Well, there's great goings-on in Wenderby!' he said. 'We don't usually get such excitement around here, I can tell you! Seems one of those scientists has been kidnapped from the Four Horseshoes. No one's talking of anything else today.'

'I'm not surprised,' said Julian. 'It was an extraordinary thing to happen!'

'And to think I saw that black car drive by!' said the garage man, neatly fitting the inner tube into the tyre. 'But I wasn't to know, was I?'

George started. 'You actually *saw* it drive by?'

'Yes, and so I told the police, but I don't know if it'll get them anywhere. However, I was able to tell them it was a Mercedes.'

'Are you sure it was the kidnappers' car?' asked Dick.

'Well, seems as if it must have been! I was on late-night duty, you see, and this road's the way to the airport, where they reckon the kidnappers would have been making for. The car was driving at a fair speed, but I could make out the driver and three men in the back. It was the only car happened to pass at that time of night.'

'And it was driving along the road to the airport, very fast?' said Dick. 'Are you sure about that too?'

The petrol pump attendant took his cap off and scratched his head. 'Yes, but now you mention it, I've thought of something else. When the car was well past, I clearly heard it slow down. It was a still night, you see, every sound was quite distinct.'

'Did it actually stop?' Anne ventured to ask.

'No, but I felt it might be about to turn off somewhere.'

'Are there any minor roads branching off this one, farther along that way?' asked Julian.

'Any amount of 'em! And lanes crossing over them too. Right, there's your wheel as good as new, then!'

Julian thanked the man, and paid him. The children got on their bikes – and set off along the road that eventually led to the airport.

'Let's go a bit further,' suggested George. 'And we'll keep our eyes open for all turnings, to right or to left. We want to take good notice of any minor road that happens to join this main one.'

They cycled quite slowly, so as not to miss anything. After about a quarter of a mile, they saw two well-trodden paths, but the ground showed nothing but the tracks of cartwheels and heavy vehicles like tractors. Timmy was running here and there, sniffing the ground, almost as if he realised what the children were doing – though *he* was more likely to be searching for rabbits than the marks of car tyres!

Then the Five reached another turning – a minor road with proper tarmac this time. They got off their bicycles again.

'Look!' said George all of a sudden. 'A car turned here not very long ago – it must have had quite new tyres, because they've left very clear track marks on the soft verge beside the road. It could have been the Mercedes!'

Encouraged by their discovery, the children turned off along this road. They wanted to go on exploring for as long as they could before Aunt Fanny would be expecting them back. The minor road along which they were now cycling was quite wide, and in good repair. It occurred to Dick that the driver of the car whose tracks they had seen must have been in a tearing hurry if he turned so abruptly that he went on to the verge beside the road like that.

'Well, yes,' said George. 'If it was the kidnappers in that car, they *would* have been in a hurry to get into cover, along with their victim.'

She still felt certain that the kidnapped Professor couldn't be far away.

The children cycled on for about another mile, and then they came to a crossroads.

'Bother!' said Dick. 'Do you think they went straight on, or turned off, and if they turned off, did they go right or left?'

Anne sighed. 'It looks as if we've lost the trail,'

she said. 'We can't go in three directions at once!'

'Oh yes, we can!' cried George. 'Why not? There are four of us, after all. Listen, Julian, why don't you and Anne take the left-hand turning? And Dick can go straight ahead, and Timmy and I will turn right. And we all meet back here to report in an hour's time. All right, everyone?'

'All right!' said her cousins – even Anne, who was beginning to feel rather tired by now. But she knew Julian would look after her. So they separated, and set off along their respective minor roads.

Dick was pedalling along, keeping his eyes well down, and he had not gone far when he noticed a patch of oil on the road. It had almost dried out, and it bore the imprint of what looked like a brand new car tyre! Jumping off his bike, Dick crouched down to take a good look.

Yes, there could be no doubt about it – Dick was observant about such things, and he was sure that the tracks were the same as the tracks on the tyres of the car they were trying to trace!

Chapter Seven

RAINBOW HOUSE

'My word!' said Dick, whistling softly. 'Now I wonder how I can let the others know? I don't want to wait a whole hour – especially as they can't be very far off yet. Oh, I know!'

Dick had had a good idea. George had not cycled very far when she suddenly heard shrill whistling. Three short notes, three long ones, three more short ones. In Morse code, that meant SOS! And there was no doubt about it, the sounds must be coming from the whistle Dick always had in his pocket, along with all sorts of other useful odds and ends.

'Timmy, did you hear that?' she asked. 'Dick's in danger! Quick, we must go and help him.'

She turned round and raced back to the cross-roads, arriving there at the same moment as Julian and Anne, who had heard their brother's distress signal too.

'Something must have happened to Dick!' cried Anne in alarm. 'Listen – he's whistling again! Oh dear, I do hope he's all right!'

'Well, at least he can't be dead yet if he's whistling as loud as all that!' said George cheerfully.

The three other children and Timmy soon caught up with Dick along the road he had chosen. They were rather surprised to find him standing by the roadside by himself, apparently perfectly safe and sound, but in a state of great excitement.

'Sorry if I scared you,' he said at once, 'but it was the only way I could get in touch before you were out of earshot. Look what I've found!'

And he pointed to the tyre mark on the patch of oil.

George whistled through her teeth. 'Oh, well done, Dick! So now we know the kidnappers went straight ahead!'

'*If* it was the kidnappers in that car!' Julian reminded her, sensible as ever. 'Don't forget, this is sheer theory! We could be quite wrong.'

'Oh, don't be such a bore, Julian!' George told him. 'It *may* be just a theory, but this is no moment to cast doubt on it, is it?'

Julian couldn't help laughing. 'All right, forget I said anything!' he said good-humouredly.

'Right, on we go then!' said George.

The children cycled another two miles, without seeing anything but small lanes turning off the road – lanes which didn't really look wide enough for a big car. Then they came to a village nestling among the hills. It looked a very pretty place, with the springtime green of all the new leaves coming out. A few farms and houses stood among the trees.

The children got off their bicycles. 'Do we go through the village and on along the road?' asked Anne. She would have liked to linger there. It seemed such a nice, quiet, peaceful place.

'No, I don't think we should go on just yet,' Julian said. 'Whether the black car went straight on, or whether it stopped in this village, somebody may have noticed it – and if they did, they might be able to give us some information. I think we could do with a nice cool drink for our elevenses, too! So let's go and find one, and we can ask some questions at the same time. I expect there's a tea-shop or something like that nearby.'

Sure enough, they found a nice little teashop in the middle of the village. There was nobody in it at the moment, and the Five sat down and ordered buns and lemonade, with a bowl of cool water for Timmy. The proprietress herself served them.

'What a nice village this looks!' George said, hoping to start up a conversation.

'Yes, Liddertoft is a pretty place – we get a good many tourists passing through in summer,' said the teashop owner.

'Are there many tourists at this time of year?' asked Dick.

The woman chuckled. 'Except for you and the people who've rented Rainbow House, I haven't seen a single new face here this spring!'

George felt her heartbeat quicken! They were really in luck today! Not only did the teashop owner seem quite happy to chat to them, but the conversation was going just the way she had hoped it might!

'Rainbow House! That's a pretty name!' she said. 'Is it a big house?'

'Quite a fair size, yes – it's out beyond the village, Muddleton way.'

'It sounds like a secluded sort of spot,' said Julian thoughtfully. 'I hope the people renting it have a car so that they can do their shopping and go sight-seeing!'

'Oh, they've got a car all right!' said the teashop lady. 'A very handsome car it is, too!'

'What make?' asked Dick eagerly. 'I'm awfully interested in cars!'

The teashop owner chuckled. 'What lad of your age isn't? But I'm afraid I don't know much about them myself. I've only noticed the gentlemen go about in a very fine black car.'

Dick's eyes were shining. But it was Anne's turn to get her question in first. 'You said "gentlemen"

– you mean there aren't any ladies or any children who ride about in it?'

'No, dear, just the three gentlemen,' said the teashop owner. 'They've only been here a few days. Come for the sake of their health, they said in the village, though they look pretty hefty, healthy fellows to me! Still, it's true the air's good up here in the fells. My husband, now, he always says . . .'

George interrupted, since the talkative teashop owner looked like getting off the subject which really interested her. 'You seem to know everything that goes on in Liddertoft!' she said.

The teashop lady chuckled comfortably. 'I should just about think I do! A little place like this, where people are always dropping in for a nice cup of tea, is quite an information bureau! And as for Rainbow House, why, the owner gave my husband the keys and asked him to be his agent and let it out, so you can be sure I know all about *that*!'

George almost asked what the tenants of Rainbow House were like, besides being "hefty, healthy fellows", but then she thought better of it. She didn't want to seem so inquisitive that this helpful lady would get suspicious.

It was time to leave, and George emptied her glass. 'That was delicious lemonade!' she said.

The teashop owner smiled, pleased, and took the money Julian offered her, assuring the children that the lemonade and the buns were all home-

made. Then the children said goodbye, and went to get on their bikes again.

George looked at her watch. 'Eleven-thirty!' she said, sighing. 'We've come quite a way, and we have to get back in time for lunch, or my mother will be worrying.'

'Yes, we must start home,' Anne agreed. The last thing she wanted to do was worry kind Aunt Fanny.

'But perhaps we've just got time to take a look at Rainbow House. I mean, it would be silly to leave this village without even setting eyes on the place that may be the kidnappers' hide-out!'

'We'll be late, though,' said Julian, 'and not to mention worrying Aunt Fanny, Uncle Quentin said he'd be back from the conference for lunch. And you know how cross *he'll* be!'

'Never mind,' said George cheerfully, 'we can tell him you had a puncture, which is quite true, and he can't hold that against us! No, Julian, please don't lecture me! Come on, we're only wasting time! Look, there's a signpost. It points that way to Muddleton.'

The children cycled out of Liddertoft along the Muddleton road. As they were leaving the village, they stopped to ask a boy exactly where Rainbow House was. In fact it wasn't as far away as Julian had feared – only about quarter of a mile. It stood well back from the road, at the end of a long path.

The garden was surrounded by a wall, with broken glass on top. There was a garage outside the wall, to the right of the house. The children ventured to go up the path. The whole place seemed perfectly silent.

'Almost like a fortress, isn't it?' whispered George.

Dick bent down to look at the end of the path and uttered a soft exclamation. 'I say! More tyre marks! And it's still the same car. There are footprints over there too – footprints of someone who went in through the front gate, while the car itself was put away in the garage beside the wall.'

'That's good observation, Dick,' Julian told his brother. 'Right – now let's be off! We don't want anyone who happens to be in that house to spot us. We can think what to do next later.'

The children cycled back to Wenderby Fell Cottage as fast as they could, but even so, Aunt Fanny and Uncle Quentin had finished their own lunch by the time the Five arrived. However, the true tale of Julian's puncture meant they were spared the lecture Uncle Quentin had been planning to give them, and anyway he had other things on his mind, and had to get back to the afternoon session of his conference.

'But you can stay in the village for once, this afternoon!' he told the children. 'I don't want your poor aunt wondering where you may have got to the whole time!'

George and her cousins didn't really mind. They had plenty to occupy their minds, and besides, it had been quite a strenuous morning. They went out for a stroll in the village, to discuss the results of their inquiries so far.

'To sum it all up,' said George, 'we suspect that Professor Allan's kidnappers took him away in a black Mercedes, and drove him to Rainbow House, where they're probably still keeping him prisoner.'

'Only *probably*,' Julian reminded her. 'And *possibly* is more like it! We have no real proof yet, remember?'

'We'll have to go back to Liddertoft to look for some. First, we want to make sure there really is a black Mercedes there, and second, we want to make sure Professor Allan really is being kept prisoner at Rainbow House.'

Anne spoke up, in her quiet little voice. 'Even if we do see a black Mercedes, that doesn't absolutely prove it's the kidnappers' car.'

'Good point, Anne,' said Julian. 'And just *how* do we find out about Professor Allan? I don't suppose, if he *is* there, he's in any position to lean out of the window waving a handkerchief and shouting, "Come along, you Five, buck up and rescue me!"

George didn't even smile at the comical picture Julian had conjured up. She was thinking.

'I know!' she said. 'What we need is something the Professor has touched a good deal!'

Dick whistled. 'I see what you mean! That's a good idea, George. We can go back to Rainbow House with this something, whatever it is, give it to Timmy to smell, and then good old Timmy will be able to tell us whether Professor Allan's really inside the house.'

'My dog is absolutely infallible when he's on the scent of something!' George said proudly.

Julian smiled. 'I agree with you there, George! So it's up to Timmy to continue the inquiries, then. We all get a turn occasionally, don't we, Timmy, old boy?'

'Woof!' said Timmy, wagging his tail.

Now all they had to decide was when to go back to Liddertoft.

'This evening!' said George at once.

'This evening?' repeated her cousins in chorus, rather doubtfully.

'Well, *I* think that's the best thing to do, and I'll tell you why!'

'Go ahead, George!' said Julian. 'Not that I think there'd be much chance of stopping you!'

Ignoring this sarcastic remark, George went on. 'First of all, we'll have plenty of time after supper – we won't have to bother about getting back late for a meal again. And we won't be so noticeable after dark as in the daylight. The tenants of Rainbow

House won't even notice if we scout around. In fact, they may even be asleep, which would give us much more freedom of action.'

'Oh, George!' gasped Anne. 'You're not thinking of actually going *into* the enemy camp, are you?'

'Well, I'm not quite sure yet just what I think we ought to do,' George admitted. 'I think we'll have to play it by ear. And now let's have a rest, shall we? Then, when we've gone upstairs to bed, we'll be feeling fresh and wide awake, and we can slip out of the house on the quiet.' George didn't like disobeying her parents, but as she told her cousins again, she felt that the end justified the means.

So after the quiet, restful afternoon, the children were all ready for an adventurous expedition after dark. Julian, always the most sensible of them, was still wondering whether it wouldn't be a better idea to go straight to the police with their suspicions of Rainbow House and its tenants. But George was anxious to have something more in the way of evidence, and wouldn't agree to Julian's suggestion.

'The police are already at work on the case anyway, remember!' she said. 'They can go about it in their own way – and we'll go about it in ours. And there's another thing, Ju: the kidnappers won't be as wary of children as policemen. I expect they're keeping an eye open all the time for any police officers, but they won't be looking out for *us*. So we have a better chance of success!'

Julian saw the point of that, and the Five set off at ten o'clock, when it was dark. Quiet as shadows, they cycled down the road. Timmy wasn't running along beside his mistress this time. George thought he had better travel in his basket on the carrier of her bike.

After about three miles' ride, the children came to Liddertoft. This time they cycled straight through the sleeping village without even slowing down. Just before reaching Rainbow House, they dismounted and left their bicycles in the ditch.

All of a sudden Dick exclaimed in dismay. 'Oh no! We've forgotten to bring something belonging to Professor Allan! What idiots we are!'

'Speak for yourself!' said George, rather smugly. '*We* didn't forget. Did we, Anne?'

Anne was laughing. 'No, we didn't. I went to get what we need before supper.'

She produced a little plastic bag from her pocket, and took a sock out of the bag. Dick and Julian stared.

'One of the Professor's socks?' said Julian. 'How on earth did you get hold of that?'

Anne smiled. 'Oh, it wasn't very difficult,' she said. 'I went to the Four Horseshoes. It's quite easy to get into the hotel without being noticed. There are so many people coming and going, I expect I looked as though I was the daughter of somebody staying there. I waited for the clerk at the reception desk to turn his back, and then I went down to the hotel basement. I had a story all ready, in case somebody stopped me and asked awkward questions, but I didn't meet anyone. I even found the laundry room and the dirty linen basket quite easily.'

'The dirty linen basket?' said Dick.

'That's right,' George told him. 'Hotels do their customers' laundry if they're asked to, and so it doesn't get all mixed up together, they put the clothes in the big basket into separate bags, labelled with the customers' names.'

'You mean Anne fished Professor Allan's sock out of one of those laundry bags?'

'That's right,' said Anne, with her sweetest smile. 'The bag had his name on it. George and I decided nobody was going to be suspicious of a young girl like me, even if I *was* found down there. I could just have said I'd lost my way.'

The two boys couldn't help laughing.

'Ssh!' said George. 'Don't forget we're on the warpath! Hand me that sock, Anne. I want to let Timmy sniff it.'

Timmy was taking his part in all this very seriously. He sniffed, sniffed and sniffed again – and then he sneezed, almost as if to tell the children he knew what they wanted. So then George pointed to Rainbow House, which could be seen looming up in the dark ahead of them, led Timmy towards the house, and whispered, 'Go on, Timmy! Seek! Good dog – seek!'

Nose to the ground, Timmy made straight for the garden gate. Once he reached it, he sniffed very loudly indeed, and tried to get past the gate to go on following the scent on the other side!

'You see?' said George triumphantly. 'He's on the trail all right. Professor Allan must be in there somewhere.'

However, the bars of the forged iron gate were too close together for Timmy to get through – and before George could stop him, the disappointed dog let out a low howl.

'Stop it, Timmy! Quiet!' George told him in alarm. 'You'll give us away!'

She was quite right! Timmy had only just stopped howling when the children heard the sound of running feet somewhere inside the wall which surrounded Rainbow House and its grounds. At the same time, they heard frantic barking. Two enormous bulldogs raced up to the gate and stopped there, jumping up at the bars and barking furiously. They were making so much noise that they were bound to rouse the tenants of the house.

'That's torn it!' muttered Julian. 'We're done for now!'

'Not yet!' said George. 'Quick – you three go back to the bikes. Timmy, you stay here and keep barking! Yes, I know I told you to be quiet, but now I *want* you to bark. That's it – good dog, keep on barking!'

Julian, Dick and Anne ran back to the place where they had left their bicycles. Meanwhile, George hid behind a bush. She heard a man's gruff voice.

'What's all this noise? Rocky! Buster! Down! You don't need to kick up that fuss just for some stray mongrel passing by! As for you, get out, you brute!' he added, obviously speaking to Timmy.

George gave a very soft whistle, to call Timmy back to her side, and the two of them stole silently away. Thanks to her clever trick, they had escaped notice even though the alarm had been raised!

'Well,' she said, when she had rejoined her cousins, 'at least we know more now. We know the place is guarded by two big dogs at night. So we'll have to be careful – and come back in daylight, when I hope the dogs will be shut up!'

'Meanwhile, we've come all this way for nothing,' said Dick gloomily. 'All that trouble, slipping out of the house on the quiet – and after all, tonight's expedition has been a failure.'

'Not entirely,' said George. 'After all, we can be quite sure Professor Allan *is* beyond the garden gate of Rainbow House! Timmy's made that clear enough. Those men must be keeping him prisoner inside the house.'

On the way back, Julian once again suggested going to the police, but George was most unwilling to do that.

'Look at it this way,' she begged her cousin. 'Professor Allan is in the hands of those kidnappers. If they see the police come swarming round the house, his jailers might panic and do him some kind of injury. We mustn't risk putting his life in danger. But if we go about it cleverly, we may be able to set him free ourselves. Then, if we don't succeed, there'll still be time to go to the police. All right?'

Rather reluctantly, Julian agreed, and the Five were soon back at Wenderby Fell Cottage. They tiptoed upstairs to bed, where they slept very soundly until next day – and not surprisingly they woke later than usual!

Chapter Eight

ON THE PROFESSOR'S TRAIL

Next morning, George asked Aunt Fanny if they could have a picnic lunch. 'We want to spend the day out of doors – we thought we'd go over to a pretty village we've found called Liddertoft,' she explained.

Aunt Fanny was quite happy to give them a picnic, and they set off with plenty of sandwiches and a big bag of apples, as well as a slab of fruit cake. What with waking up late, and having to wait while Aunt Fanny prepared the picnic, the Five didn't reach Liddertoft until lunch-time. Julian saw a meadow beside a little stream outside the village, on the Muddleton road.

'Let's stop and have our picnic here,' he suggested. 'We can discuss our plan of attack while we eat it.'

It was easy enough to decide what they wanted

to do – get inside Rainbow House, to find out more about the enemy there. The question was, *how*? George thought of a clever trick which would lull any suspicions the kidnappers might have.

'We'll go and play ball with Timmy just outside the garden gate of Rainbow House,' she said. 'And I'll throw the ball over the wall, as if by accident. Then all I have to do is ring the bell and ask politely if I can go in and get my ball back.'

'They won't let you,' said Dick. 'At best they'll go and find it for you, but they won't let you in.'

'I'll make sure I get in somehow!' said George.

'Nothing venture, nothing win!' said Anne, rather surprisingly.

'Well said, Anne!' George agreed. 'Come on, then, everybody!'

The children packed up their picnic things and made for Rainbow House, followed by Timmy. Soon they had a lively game of ball going on the grass outside the wall. They kept shouting to each other, Timmy was leaping about and barking, and altogether they made a good deal of cheerful, happy noise. Even the most suspicious person couldn't have guessed that this innocent game was just camouflage for a clever plan.

All of a sudden, George let out a cry of dismay. 'Oh dear! My ball's gone over the wall!'

'You clumsy thing!' shouted Dick, at the top of his voice. 'Go and get it back, and hurry up!'

'I will – if there's anyone living in this house, that is!' said George, in as loud a voice as her cousin's. 'I suppose I can always try ringing the bell!'

And she pulled the chain hanging by the gateway. Inside the garden, a bell rang, and almost at once a man appeared at the gate – perhaps he had been listening on the other side of the wall! He didn't open the gate, but looked at the children through the bars.

'Did you ring the bell, young man?' he asked George. Like so many other people, he thought she was a boy, with her short hair, jeans and boyish manner.

'Yes, sir,' she said, sounding apologetic. 'We were playing a game, and I'm afraid I threw our ball over the wall of your garden. Could I come in and find it?'

'No, just wait there and I'll get it for you,' said the man. But then he looked round him, and seemed to hesitate. There were a great many tangled shrubs and bushes on the garden side of the wall, as George could see for herself now. He obviously didn't want to spend time searching them! Much to her relief, he thought better of his decision and said, 'Oh, all right, come in and look for the ball yourself. I'll give you five minutes!'

George glanced triumphantly at her cousins, and went through the gate, which the man opened for her.

'Can we come in and help?' asked Dick, hopefully.

'No, you other kids wait there,' said the man. He practically slammed the gate shut in Dick's face. George wasted no time. Bent over, she pretended to be looking for her ball, but really she was taking in all she could of the surroundings, trying to impress details on her mind. She saw the house, counted its doors and windows, took note of the stone steps up to the front door, the big oak tree growing just to the right of the house, the lawn, which wouldn't make any sound underfoot as you walked over it . . .

Suddenly a voice with a slight foreign accent made her turn her head.

'What is it, Martin? What's going on? Why did you let that boy in?'

The man who had just appeared on the steps outside the house was tall and well dressed. His eyes were as cold as his tone of voice.

'Sorry, sir,' said the man addressed as Martin. 'The boy threw his ball over the wall.'

'Well, send him packing, and then get the car out. I want you to drive me into town.'

And the man turned and went into the house, while the other man, called Martin, who was obviously the chauffeur, quickly showed George out again.

'Too bad about your ball!' he said brusquely. 'You shouldn't have been playing so close to the house!'

The gate closed behind her with a click, and Martin disappeared. The children went meekly away – but there was a light of triumph in George's eyes! Once they were out of earshot, she said, 'We've done it! I saw everything there was to see! I made a mental note of the way the place looks inside the wall, and sure enough, the bulldogs weren't around. They must be kept shut up during the day.' She laughed, and added, 'What a bit of luck the other man came along, and I didn't get the ball back!'

'Why?' asked Julian, surprised.

'Well, it means we've got a good excuse if anyone finds us in the garden of Rainbow House! We've come to look for our ball!'

'George, you're not really thinking of going back inside there in broad daylight, are you?' said Julian.

'Yes, of course I am,' George replied. 'After all, we can't get in at night. And you heard what that kidnapper said – he and the chauffeur are going off in the car. So work it out: two kidnappers plus one chauffeur plus one prisoner makes four people. Four people minus one kidnapper minus one chauffeur makes one kidnapper and one prisoner. See? What I'm driving at is that we'll only have one enemy to deal with.'

'But there may be *more* than three men guarding the Professor,' Dick objected.

'I'll be very surprised if there are,' said George. 'They won't want to draw attention to themselves. Any more than three men, and the local people would start asking questions about what they wanted to hire the house for.'

'What exactly are you planning to do, George?' asked Anne.

'Wait here behind this hedge. And as soon as we've seen the spies' car leave, we'll get over the wall, trying not to be seen ourselves, and then we'll decide what to do,' said George.

'But suppose we *are* seen?' asked Julian.

'We just say we are looking for our ball – we might be thrown out double quick, but that's the worst that's likely to happen.'

'Hm – oh, well, I suppose it's worth trying,' said Julian. 'But I don't want Dick and Anne coming in, George. They can stay outside with Timmy, and I'll come in with you.'

The children had only ten minutes to wait. A car soon drove out of the garage of Rainbow House towards the road. Sure enough, it was a black Mercedes!

'Come on, then!' said George.

The Five made for the house. Julian chose the part of the wall which he thought was least likely to be visible from the house, threw his anorak up to cover the broken glass on top, and took a run. He managed to haul himself up to the top of the wall without doing himself any harm except for a slight graze on the wrist. Sitting astride his anorak, which protected him from the glass, he helped George up too. Then they both jumped down into the garden, and stood perfectly still for a moment. If they'd been seen, or if the bulldogs had got wind of them, that would be the end of their adventure. But nothing happened.

'I've got an idea, Julian,' George whispered to her cousin. 'Come on!'

George was seldom short of ideas! Bending over so as to keep close to the ground, the two children made their way to the foot of the big oak which towered above the house.

'Let's climb it!' said George. 'I'm sure we'll be able to see into several rooms of the house from up there!'

She and Julian were soon clambering up into the branches of the tree. Then, all of a sudden, Julian stopped. 'Look!' he whispered. 'See that?'

He pointed to a window standing wide open, opposite the part of the big oak tree they had reached. The children, well hidden among the leaves, could see right into the room – and they were in luck! It seemed to be a bedroom, and there were two men inside it.

One of the men was sitting on a chair at a table covered with sheets of blank paper. The other man was standing in front of him, and the two cousins could hear this second man's voice quite clearly.

'Come along, make an effort, can't you?' he was saying. 'Have another go at those calculations of yours. We want that formula in black and white, and then no harm will come to you. Otherwise – well, you'd better watch out! We're beginning to lose patience, you know. Don't forget, this situation can't last for ever. If you don't come up with that formula within the next two days, we'll be getting out of the country, come what may – and so will you, Professor! And we'll be handing you over to some people whose methods are much tougher than anything I and my friends have used. They'll know how to make you reveal the secret of your discovery, you may be sure of that!'

'See that? He's got a pistol!' George whispered in Julian's ear. 'We guessed right! Those men are trying to make the Professor tell them the plans for making his Z-ray transmitter!'

'You think the man at the table is Professor Allan?'

'Yes, of course – who else would he be? Anyway, I've seen him before. He once came to see my father. How can we rescue him?'

'Ssh!' said Julian. 'Look!'

Inside the room, the Professor had angrily swept the sheets of blank paper to the floor. 'I am not

going to write anything at all!' he said firmly. 'It's no good threatening me like that. My invention is mine alone – and no business of yours!'

The spy did not lose his temper. Instead, he made the Professor get up and lie down on the bed. Then he fastened him down with a complicated system of leather straps, keeping the pistol pointing at him all the time, and after that he left the room.

Julian and George scrambled down from their perch in the oak tree, went back to Dick and Anne, and told them what they had seen.

'Oh, how terrible!' cried Anne. 'That poor Professor! And there's nothing we can do to help him!'

'Yes, there is!' said Julian. 'We can go to the police, that's what!'

George tapped her foot impatiently. 'Oh, Julian how many more times do I have to tell you? Those spies are obviously determined to do anything, however desperate, to keep their prisoner in their own hands! A sudden police raid might make them kill the Professor in a moment of panic! They might not mean to – they're so keen to get their hands on the Paralyser – but accidents do happen.'

Then she calmed down all of a sudden, and a smile appeared on her lips.

'I've got an idea!' said George.

Even at a moment like this, her cousins couldn't help laughing.

'Not another!' said Dick sarcastically. 'I hope it's a good one, that's all!'

'I *think* it is,' said George, perfectly seriously. 'Listen, I want you three to stay here, behind this hedge, and wait for me. I've got to go back to Wenderby Fell Cottage, but I'll be back here again as soon as I possibly can!'

'Back to Wenderby Fell Cottage?' asked Julian. 'Whatever for?'

'Sorry – no time to explain just now!' said George. 'I've got about six miles to cycle, going there and back! You keep watch while I'm gone – and you can wait here too, Timmy! Right, I'm off!'

And she jumped on her bike and pedalled away at high speed, leaving her three puzzled cousins behind her.

The sun was hot, and cycling fast was tiring, but all the same George did the journey back to Wenderby Fell Cottage in record time. On the way, she thought of what the word "paralyser" had suggested to her when she used it to her cousins just now.

'My father still has that experimental transmitter,' she said to herself. 'The one we got back from the local burglars! I don't know whether the police let him take it away because he's one of the most important scientists at the conference, or because the thing's as safe with him as it could be anywhere – but what I *do* know is where he's hidden it. It's at the bottom of the old coal scuttle down in the cellar of Wenderby Fell Cottage. Nobody would think of looking for it there – except me! And when I've got it, I ought to be able to rescue its inventor!'

That was George's new idea! She planned to borrow the Allan Paralyser and use it to outwit the people who wanted to get hold of it themselves!

When she got back to the cottage, George left her bicycle at the garden gate and went down to the cellar. Luckily Aunt Fanny seemed to be busy somewhere else, and didn't see her come in. Before she left again, George went into the room her father was using as a study, and did something there too. She left the room with a small smile on her lips. And when she set off for Liddertoft once more, the experimental Paralyser was in Timmy's basket on her carrier, well strapped down and hidden under a stout piece of tarpaulin.

Julian, Dick and Anne were pleased and relieved to see George back again. Timmy managed not to bark, sensing that his mistress would rather he didn't, but he jumped up and licked her cheek lovingly.

'All right, all right, old boy!' gasped George, rather breathlessly. 'Well, did anything happen while I was gone?'

As she spoke to her cousins, she was undoing the package she had brought back with her.

'I'm afraid something *did* happen,' Dick told her. 'A bit of bad luck, in fact. The car came back. So now there are three people to deal with!'

'Never mind!' said George, smiling broadly. '*This* should take care of Martin and his bosses!'

'The Allan Paralyser!' Julian exclaimed.

'The Allan Paralyser!' said Dick and Anne at almost the same time.

'That's right – armed with this, we ought to be safe enough. Julian, could you and Dick go and rescue the Professor? Anne can stay here and –'

'No, I can't! I'm coming with you!' said Anne firmly.

'Woof!' said Timmy, speaking up for himself.

The bit of tarpaulin with which George had covered the Z-ray transmitter came in very useful – the children put it over the broken glass on top of the wall so that they could climb over without hurting themselves. They had to haul Timmy up too. And then, at the vital moment, their luck seemed to change! Dick was the last to climb the wall, and was sitting astride it, just about to jump down into the garden, when they suddenly heard a voice quite close.

'Hallo, what's this? Breaking in, are you? Bunch of young thieves!'

It was Martin the chauffeur! George didn't give her cousins any chance to answer back, though. She smiled at the man.

'Oh, we're not thieves!' she said. 'In fact, we've come to bring you something you want very much indeed!'

As she spoke, she pressed the red button of the Paralyser. Martin was rooted to the spot at once, and stood there motionless with his mouth open!

Dick jumped down from the top of the wall, laughing. There they were, all five of them, safe in the garden of Rainbow House, with one of their enemies out of action already!

'Come on!' said Julian.

They marched towards the house, and had just reached the front steps when the door suddenly opened. The man Julian and George had seen in the prisoner's room stood there. He must have seen them coming.

'What the –?' he began. But he got no further. The Allan Paralyser had interrupted him in mid-sentence.

'And that makes two!' said Dick happily.

'Oh, quick, let's go and find the poor Professor!' said Anne.

The children ran up the stairs leading to the first floor. They met the other spy on the landing. He had no time to express his fury and astonishment either – because next moment *he* was immobilised in front of the children's eyes!

'Professor Allan!' shouted Julian. 'Where are you? We've come to rescue you!'

The Professor called back to him, and his voice guided the children to the room where they found the poor man strapped down to a bed.

'Oh, Professor Allan!' said George. 'We're so glad to see you! Listen – I'm Quentin Kirrin's daughter, and you'll be free in a moment now!'

'My dear children!' said the amazed Professor. 'I don't know how to thank you!'

'It's your own invention you have to thank, sir!' said Julian, and George showed him the Paralyser. 'We managed to get in here and put your captors out of action thanks to that transmitter!'

'Good heavens!' said the Professor. And then Julian and Dick got to work on the straps tying him down – or tried to. It was a complicated system, with metal fastenings, which must be easy to operate if only you knew how! The two boys broke several fingernails on it in their impatience. And still they hadn't managed to set the Professor free.

'Oh, this is stupid!' said George impatiently. 'Here, let me have a go!'

She put the Z-ray transmitter down on the table, and tried undoing the fastenings herself. So did Anne. Timmy watched the operation with interest. Several minutes passed by, and at last Dick managed to free the prisoner's legs.

'Do be as quick as you can!' Professor Allan begged them. 'If the effects wear off, and those men – oh!'

His exclamation of alarm was uttered at the sight of the chauffeur Martin arriving in the room, silent and menacing, with a pistol in his hand. The man stood there in the doorway. Obviously the effects of the Paralyser *had* worn off – and he looked very ready to take his revenge! Before the startled children could take action, he reached out and picked up the Allan Paralyser from the table! Timmy growled and bared his teeth.

'Ssh, Timmy!' George whispered. She was furious with herself for putting the transmitter down! Now that Martin was "unparalysed" again, the two spies would soon be joining him. Not only had the Five failed to free the Professor, they were all in the enemy's hands – *and* they had made the spies a present of the Allan Paralyser itself!

'And it's all my fault!' George said to herself angrily. 'Oh, what a fool I am! I should have realised something like this might happen.'

It was not often that George admitted to being in the wrong, but this time she knew she had made a mistake. The Professor sighed sadly. Dick, Julian and Anne looked at their cousin, and George thought they must be blaming her. Timmy pressed himself against her for comfort. But it wasn't much comfort to think that for once the Five had been outwitted.

Suddenly the two spies burst into the room – looking really furious. However, when they saw the Paralyser in Martin's hands, they relaxed. They said something to each other in a language the children didn't understand, and then smiled at them!

'Thank you, young people!' said one of them. 'You've brought us exactly what we wanted. Very well, Martin, tie those brats up, knock the dog out, and get the car ready. It seems we had better leave this place a little earlier than we'd planned. We'll take these children with us, as hostages, in case we're stopped on our way. The police will hardly fire on a car full of innocent children!'

Horrified, George saw Martin walk towards Timmy, ready to knock him out with the butt of his pistol. 'Oh no – don't hurt him!' she cried. 'Use the Paralyser instead!'

'Yes, we might as well,' said one of the spies, picking the transmitter up. 'It will save time!'

And then, just as he raised his arm to point the Paralyser at Timmy, a voice out on the landing snapped, 'Hands up or we fire! You there – yes, you, holding that transmitter – put it down on the table. If you don't, you'll get a bullet through the head before you can turn it on us!'

Quivering with rage, but powerless to do anything about it, the spy obeyed. George rushed forward and grabbed the transmitter with a cry of delight. Julian, Dick and Anne, as pleased as she was, watched a small troop of men walk into the room. There were several uniformed police officers, three plainclothes detectives – and Uncle Quentin himself!

The man who had spoken to the spies was the police sergeant from Wenderby, whom the children already knew.

'Put the handcuffs on them!' he told his men.

Uncle Quentin was already leaning over the Professor's bed, deftly undoing the fastenings of the straps. Timmy, realising that the danger was over, started leaping happily around George. Julian, Dick and Anne were looking at their cousin.

'Well, old girl!' said Julian. 'All's well that ends well, and so forth, but you must admit we very nearly failed this time!'

'Not as nearly as you think!' murmured George, with a little smile.

'What do you mean?' asked Dick.

'Honestly,' said George, 'you don't seem to think I've got any sense at all! When I'd picked up the Allan Paralyser, I went to Father's study, wrote a note and left it where he'd be sure to find it, explaining where we were and what we were going to do – and confessing that I'd borrowed the transmitter. I thought that would be the most sensible thing to do – *and* the most honest thing to do as well.'

'Well done, George!' said Julian, generously.

'Thought of everything, didn't you?' said Dick, teasing George just a little.

'Well, she did, and she was quite right!' said loyal Anne. 'She came out on top!'

'*We* came out on top!' said George. And – 'Woof!' said Timmy, backing her up.

Uncle Quentin interrupted the children's conversation. He didn't look quite as stern as they might have feared.

'Well, the plainclothes men who came here with us will look after the kidnappers,' he said. 'And the Wenderby police have kindly said they'll pick up your bicycles and leave them at the cottage. I think we can all get into my car – it's waiting outside.'

'But first, my dear Kirrin, I want to thank your daughter and her cousins and congratulate them!' said Professor Allan, warmly. He shook hands with all the children – and shook paws with Timmy too. After all, it was the good dog who had found the prisoner's scent and put the children on his trail!

As Uncle Quentin was driving his happy carload back to Wenderby, George suddenly started laughing.

'You know, I don't really think the Four Horseshoes Hotel, where you're staying, deserves its name!' she told Professor Allan. 'I mean, a horseshoe is supposed to be lucky! But you didn't have much luck staying there. If you ask me, they ought to give that hotel a new name and call it the Ill Winds, or the Unlucky Thirteen, or something like that!'

And the case of the Z-rays and the Allan Paralyser ended in fits of laughter!

If you have enjoyed this book you may like to read some more exciting adventures from Knight Books. Here is a complete list of Enid Blyton's **FAMOUS FIVE** adventures:

1. Five on a Treasure Island
2. Five go Adventuring Again
3. Five Run Away Together
4. Five go to Smuggler's Top
5. Five go off in a Caravan
6. Five go to Kirrin Island Again
7. Five go off to Camp
8. Five get into Trouble
9. Five fall into Adventure
10. Five on a Hike Together
11. Five have a Wonderful Time
12. Five go down to the Sea
13. Five go to Mystery Moor
14. Five have Plenty of Fun
15. Five on a Secret Trail
16. Five go to Billycock Hill
17. Five get into a Fix
18. Five on Finniston Farm
19. Five go to Demon's Rocks
20. Five have a Mystery to Solve
21. Five are Together Again